TROUT AND ME

SUSAN SHREVE

A DELL YEARLING BOOK

Published by
Dell Yearling
an imprint of
Random House Children's Books
a division of Random House, Inc.
New York

Visit us on the Web! www.randomhouse.com/kids

Educators and librarians, for a variety of teaching tools, visit us at
www.randomhouse.com/teachers

ISBN: 0-440-41902-6

Reprinted by arrangement with Alfred A. Knopf

Printed in the United States of America

July 2004

10 9 8 7 6 5 4 3 2 1

OPM

FOR A DIFFERENT BEN—
THE AMAZING BENJAMIN RICHARDS

THANKS TO MY WONDERFUL EDITOR,
NANCY HINKEL, AND AGENT, JENNIE DUNHAM,
AND TO JEFF AND CONNIE FOR BRINGING
TO OUR FAMILY, AMONG OTHER PRIZES,
TWO REMARKABLE KIDS.

CHAPTER ONE

This Monday, my last week of sixth grade, I was walking up the front steps of Stockton Elementary School and there was Trout. I was sure it was Trout. It had to be and my heart flipped over. He was standing at the top of the steps in front of the double green doors, looking around for me like he used to do every morning of the fifth grade. And my heart flipped over.

"So what's up?" he used to ask.

"Not much," I'd reply.

Then he'd throw his long arm around my shoulder and we'd go in the front door of school.

"Today I was thinking of pulling the fire alarm during sixth-grade lunch," he'd say. "Whaddya think?"

"Bad idea," I'd probably say, but I'd be laughing. I was happy almost every day that Trout was at Stockton

1

Elementary, from the time he came until the end of fifth grade, and then I had to go to sixth grade without him.

I walked up to the top of the steps, hoping and hoping that I was right, but as I got closer to the boy I thought was Trout, I knew with a sinking feeling that it wasn't him at all. Just Billy Blister, who is as tall as Trout with soft blond hair, but with pimples and pink cheeks and no chin. And he is boring. Trout was never boring.

Long before Trout ever came to Stockton Elementary in Stockton, New Jersey, I'd been in trouble at school. I used to think I was an "amazing boy," like my mom said. "More or less perfect," my dad told his friends. I'd spend the days in play groups or at the petting zoo with my sister, Meg, or playing games at the park with my dad or at the circus with my mom or just hanging out kicking a ball on the blacktop behind our apartment, sometimes all by myself. And then I went to school.

I've hated school ever since first grade, when Ms. Percival got me sent home on Halloween for stuffing Mary Sue Briggs's purple teddy bear into the lower-school toilet. The toilet is located just outside the first-grade classroom because six-year-olds sometimes forget they have to pee until the last minute. The door to the toilet is usually kept closed, but on that day it happened to be open while I was pushing the bear headfirst down that long tunnel, and most of the class, including Mary Sue, were standing around the hall watching me. So it wasn't exactly a secret.

But Halloween, of all days in the year. I will never forgive Ms. Percival for that. I had my Lion King costume in my cubby to wear to the parade on the blacktop behind the school just after lunch.

Then I forgot it when the principal sent me home, and the school was locked by the time I remembered, so I had to wear my regular jeans and a black mask to go trick-or-treating.

Mary Sue Briggs deserved a wet teddy bear. Even now, five years later and in the sixth grade, I'd do the same thing again. Except now it wouldn't make any difference to Mary Sue. She doesn't have teddy bears any longer, only purple lipstick and plastic bracelets and rings with colored stones she wears on all her fingers. But she still has the same mean character she had when she was six.

"Character" is a word my father uses. I'm not exactly sure what it means. He refers to my character as "good," even though I have spent five years in nonstop trouble at school. He thinks that Mary Sue Briggs, who happens to be the best student in my class and a teacher's pet as well, is a girl of "questionable character."

"I don't get what you mean," I said, although I certainly agreed with anything bad he had to say about Mary Sue. "Everybody thinks she's perfect."

"Who is everybody?" he asked.

"The teachers like her. I mean, she plays up to them."

"Exactly," my father said.

"So is character about good guys and bad guys?" I asked.

"Sometimes the guys who are considered bad, especially at school, are actually kids of real character and the good guys like Mary Sue can't be trusted. It's worth thinking about," my father said.

He's always telling me something is worth thinking about, like I have all the time in the world to lie around my room thinking about character.

The thing I haven't told you is that I have a lisp. I've always had a lisp since I started to talk. When I was very little, like two and three and four, before I went to school, my parents and especially my sister, Meg, thought a lisp was cute.

"Say 'sweetheart,' " Meg would say to me.

I'd say "thweetheart" and Meg would laugh and call my mother, and I'd do it again and my mother would laugh, and then at dinner I'd say "thweetheart" to my father and he would laugh too. So I thought I was good at speaking and especially funny.

That lasted until kindergarten. On the first day of kindergarten, I was sitting at one of those little round tables with other kids, opening my lunch box, in which my mother had put a peanut butter and jelly sandwich with

4

the crust cut off, a thermos of vegetable soup, and a chocolate chip cookie. I told Ms. Ross, the teacher sitting next to me, that I didn't need any help screwing off the top of the thermos, but as it turned out, I was wrong. The thermos turned over, the vegetable soup went all over the table and the floor, even onto the teacher's lap, and I burst into tears. I mean, I was only five years old.

"I didn't mean to spill my thoup," I said.

"Soup," the teacher said, mopping up the mess.

I looked up at her.

"Say 'soup,' Ben," she said.

I didn't even try. I knew I couldn't say "soup," so I pretended not to hear her and jumped up from the table and ran around the classroom.

That night my mom told me she had spoken with my teacher.

"I know," I said. "She got mad at me for saying 'thoup.'"

"Not mad, sweetheart. She's a teacher and she was trying to teach you."

"Okay, thweetheart," I said, expecting her to laugh. But this time my mom didn't laugh at all. Instead, she repeated "sweetheart" like I didn't know the difference, just as Ms. Ross had done.

"So Daddy and I have decided it would be helpful if you saw a speech therapist, who will teach you to say s instead of th."

"I didn't think it wath thuch a bad thing," I said to her. "I thought it wath funny."

"It's not a bad thing," my mother said. "But now that you're in school, you need to learn to speak correctly."

So first I saw Ms. Breese and then I saw Mr. Aiken and then I saw Ms. Potter and then I saw Ms. Wade and none of them was able to teach me how to say my s's. Not even a little.

"I'm tired of speech therapists," I said to my mother. "I don't care if I lisp."

That was before I met Mary Sue Briggs, who was given the desk next to mine in Ms. Percival's first-grade classroom. Every morning she came to school with her book bag over her shoulder and her teddy bear scrunched up against her chest. She'd put her book bag in the cubby and wrap the stupid bear in a piece of fuzzy cloth, sort of like a blanket. She'd kiss its face and put it inside the desk, tell the stupid bear "night, night," and there it would stay all day until it was time to go home.

So on the day that my life turned inside out and I became known as "Ben Carter in Trouble," as if that were my whole name, we were sitting in the lunchroom, Mary Sue sitting on one side of me and Billy Bass on the other, and Billy Bass said to me, "What did you bring in your thermos?"

"Tomato thoup," I said.

"Tomato thoup?" Mary Sue asked. "I never heard of that."

"He means 'soup,' " Billy said.

"But he said 'thoup,' " Mary Sue said.

She turned to Elly Suregate on the other side of her.

"Did you hear that Ben has tomato thoup in his thermos?"

And she fell off the chair laughing. Elly was laughing too and told Tammy Anderson what I'd said, and they both laughed into the sleeves of their shirts.

"Say my name?" Mary Sue said when she could control herself.

"Rat fink," I said.

I stuffed my lunch into my lunch pail and got up from the table. I was thinking about pouring my tomato soup over Mary Sue's curly brown hair. But I didn't do that. Instead, I left the lunchroom without a word and walked down the corridor, past the third and second grades, to our first-grade classroom. Ms. Percival was at her desk correcting our spelling. I hated spelling because I was bad at it and still am, even if I memorize all the words before a test and practice and practice with Meg. Mostly I fail, so I expected Ms. Percival to give me one of her sad "you've failed *again*, Benjamin" looks, but she didn't. Instead, she looked up and smiled and said, "Hello, Ben," in that singsong voice she has. I didn't answer.

I walked over to Mary Sue Briggs's desk, lifted the top,

took out her purple teddy bear, walked right past Ms. Percival, opened the door to the first graders' bathroom, and started to stuff the bear's head into the hole at the bottom of the toilet. Then I flushed the toilet. I don't know what I thought would happen when I flushed the toilet with a bear in the bowl. I suppose I hoped that the bear would disappear into the darkness of the pipes and sewers. But what did happen is that the toilet overflowed all over my shoes and Ms. Percival's shoes and water ran down the corridor and Jonno Bailey rushed by me and pulled the bear out of the hole in the toilet bowl and gave it to Mary Sue, who was crying.

Ms. Percival gave a little screech when the water from the toilet rushed over the toes of her shoes, grabbed me by the shoulder, and took me to the principal's office, and the principal sent me home. Just like that.

I don't know what happened to the teddy bear because Mary Sue never brought him to school again. He probably sat on her bed, his lavender fur all matted, and she went to bed every night thinking bad thoughts about me.

I do know what happened in the principal's office.

The principal's name is Mr. O'Dell and I don't like him. He's one of those guys who look at you with a sorrowful expression and say that they know exactly how you feel.

"I know all about you, Ben," he'll say to me. "I was a boy once, too."

Well, he doesn't know *anything* about the way I feel and never did. If he was ever a kid, it was for less than five minutes. My guess is he was about fifty when he was born, with the same stubby little black beard and slick black hair and fleshy cheeks he's got now, only he was probably worse-looking because he was supposed to be a boy.

"So, Benjamin," Mr. O'Dell said. "As you know, you shouldn't have done that to Mary Sue's teddy bear, but I understand how you might be angry about your lisp.

"I'm sure it's also frustrating to have trouble learning to read," Mr. O'Dell continued.

This was news to me. I couldn't read very well, but I didn't know Ms. Percival had noticed that. Usually when we read out loud for the class, I told her I was having a problem with asthma. I don't have asthma, but Meg sometimes does and tells me she can't talk. She has to save her breath.

"So I'm giving your parents a call," he said, as if he were planning to invite them to the movies. "We'll have a meeting, all of us, and decide how to help you with your schoolwork, Ben."

"I don't need any help," I said. I was getting very upset. I had thought this meeting was going to be about the purple teddy bear, which would have been bad enough. And now it was turning out to be about me and my reading problems.

"You need some help in reading," Mr. O'Dell said.

"I read," I said.

He shook his head. "Reading *better*," he said. "We want you to be happy here."

"I am happy. Until today I was happy."

"But you'd be happier if you learned to read."

I decided to stop talking since we'd already had that conversation and it wasn't going to be any better the second time.

And so Mr. O'Dell called my parents. A few days later, they came to his office and we all had a meeting and it was decided that I should be tested for learning disabilities.

"What are learning disabilities?" I asked on the way home from the meeting with Mr. O'Dell.

"I'm not exactly sure, Ben," my mother said. "Children learn at different rates and Mr. O'Dell wants to find out about your rate of learning."

"Because of what I did to the teddy bear?"

"No," my mother said. "Because Ms. Percival says you're having difficulty learning to read."

"She's completely wrong."

"Maybe," my mother said. "We'll see."

My mother always says "we'll see" when she doesn't know what else to say.

"We'll see what?" I asked.

"We'll see what happens," my mother said.

Usually nothing ever happens, but this time it did. This time I went to see a special teacher at Stockton Elementary who has braces and curly hair the color of lemons. Braces and she's a grown-up. Her job was to give me tests. I was supposed to talk and talk to her and draw pictures and tell her what I saw in the pictures she showed me, like a picture of a lamb looked to me like the black Lab I wanted for my birthday and didn't get. By the time the test was over, I was so angry at Mary Sue Briggs for starting this whole mess I didn't know what to do.

And it did turn out to be a mess.

First off, the special teacher decided I *did* have learning disabilities.

"Like what?" I asked my mother.

We were sitting in the living room on the couch next to the rug where my new basset puppy, Jetty, peed almost every morning before I had a chance to let her out. My mother was trying to pretend we were having the most ordinary kind of school talk, but I could tell that she was worried.

"The tests show that you reverse your letters and you seem to have a problem with visual memory and a few other things, which we'll talk about. Nothing important."

"Then I don't need to talk about it," I said.

My father had come into the living room by then. He sat down next to me and put his hand on my knee in one of those fatherly ways and said that this kind of thing happened all the time.

"What kind of thing?" I asked.

"As far as I can tell, most normal boys in the United States have learning disabilities. I'm sure I have them too, but when I went to school, who knew a learning disability from a football."

My father talks like that sometimes. He's not a very patient man. Besides, as I told you, he cares more about "character" than grades, probably because he had trouble in school too. He told me that himself.

"So what's going to happen?" I asked my mother.

"You're going to have your own teacher to work with on reading for an hour every day."

"I don't want my own teacher," I said.

My mother didn't argue. She's smart that way. She doesn't argue with me, never even disagrees with me, but she always gets things her own way.

Which is what happened. I had a reading teacher and a speech therapist and by the time I was in the second grade, I had become what Mr. O'Dell called a *problem* child.

Since the teddy bear, everyone expected trouble from me. So that's what they got.

CHAPTER TWO

I live on Park Avenue, across the street from the pharmacy where my mother works making prescriptions and next door to the hardware store that my father owns. There aren't a lot of houses on Park Avenue, mostly businesses, but we live on the third floor of a three-floor apartment building instead of in a house in a residential area so my parents can walk to work. Sometimes I wish there were more kids in the neighborhood, since I only have my sister, Meg, who started high school this year and is my best friend in spite of her new boyfriend, Max, who I hate. But there're no kids I could be friends with in the apartment building, except Belinda on the second floor and Megan on the first, and "that's that for this," as my father would say. So it's been me and Meg since the beginning, which was the year I was born and she was five.

I would have left Stockton Elementary for someplace like Nova Scotia before the end of first grade if it weren't for Meg. Her real name is Margaret, but she's always changing it depending on how she feels. She does the same thing with her hair. Sometimes it's long with one braid or two or short and curly or dyed red or striped yellow with fringed bangs. Every week or two, she changes it. But for names, she's Meg since she met Max. Meg and Max—she likes that. Before Max she was Maggie and before that she was M.C. for Margaret Carter and before that she was Margaret, which was the name she had when I was in first grade and she was in sixth. As Margaret, she was first in her class and winner of the citizenship award and best athlete award and best student award. She wore her dark brown hair in one long braid laced with ribbons, and short skirts with tights and black high-tops. Most of the boys I knew thought she was "foxy," which was the word for *sexy* then. So I liked to walk out of the first-grade classroom when the bell for dismissal rang and up the stairs to the upper classrooms and meet Meg. We'd leave school together, sometimes with her friends, sometimes just the two of us, running down the front steps, stopping at my mother's drugstore for candy, and then lying around the living room until my parents came home with supper.

"So how's school today?" Meg would ask me once we were back in the apartment, after her friends had left.

14

"I hate it," I'd say.

That was nothing new. After Mary Sue Briggs and my "diagnosis," as Ms. Percival called the learning disabilities and my speech therapist and my special reading teacher, there was nothing during the day to like except lunch. I missed recess for speech tutoring and twice a week I missed gym for reading and by the end of first grade someone had decided that I had "eye-hand coordination" problems as well.

"Of course he has eye-hand coordination problems. He's a boy," my father said one night at dinner. "No six-year-old boy wants to sit at a desk for eight hours a day bored to death. He ought to be playing baseball."

"Roger."

The way my mother said "Roger," which is my father's name, sounded like trouble to me. As if she's saying "Don't ever speak like that in front of Ben." Or "Set a good example. You're the father, after all."

My father can't help himself. He says exactly what he thinks and that drives my mother crazy. She's a good and patient person. She tries very hard not to be upset with me, but the fact is, she doesn't like problems and a problem is what I am.

"So why do you hate school today?" Meg would ask.

It became a daily ritual with us. I'd be lying on the couch, probably eating oatmeal cookies, feeding half a cookie to Jetty and half to me, and Meg'd be lying on her stomach on the rug with her CD player on low.

I'd turn on my side, pull Jetty up on the couch with me, snug under my arm.

"So today the speech therapist came in her rabbit ears and whiskers and said 'Benny, say thweetheart,' " I'd begin. Meg loves it when I make up stories about my stupid tutors.

"And so what did you say?" Meg would ask.

"Nothing," I said. "I've stopped talking."

"That'll help your lisp."

"Since I stopped talking, it's gone away. No lithp."

"And can you read now?" Meg would ask.

"Try me."

She'd open her book bag and take out the library book she was reading, maybe eighth-grade level, maybe grown-up, open it to the first page, push it across the rug. "So read to me."

I'd put the book on my stomach and pretend to read, making up a story instead.

"Once upon a time there was a girl called Babycakes who came to school in her sister's flowered bikini under-wear and that is all she wore, even in the winter," I'd pre-tend to read. "And Babycakes was *fat*, so you could hardly see the underwear when she walked into Ms. Percival's first-grade classroom and sat down at her desk and took out her pencils and her reading book and her chocolate bar, took the paper off the chocolate bar, and ate it completely before the bell rang for first period."

"Oh, Benjamin Carter. You're such a genius," Meg would laugh. "You read perfectly."

"I know I do. I'm brilliant. A giant brain. One of a kind. Everybody says so."

"And I'm so proud you're my one and only brother," Meg would say.

But the truth was, I had a fluttery feeling in my stomach every day I walked up the front steps of the school.

By the second grade, my report cards used to read like a prison record. They were full of U's for Unsatisfactory and D's for Disrespectful, Disturbing, Difficult, Disorganized, Dumb, Dreadful, Disgusting. There were long paragraphs of recommendations for my improvement and the suggestion that I might be happier in a Montessori school.

"Honestly, Ben. You've got to pull yourself together or we'll be visiting you at the juvenile detention home," my father said. By the time I was in the fourth grade, even he had lost patience with what the teachers referred to as my Deplorable Behavior.

According to the teachers at Stockton, my Deplorable Behavior included stuff like falling over backwards in my chair during reading class or dropping Billy Blister's

sunglasses, which he wears to show off, in the trash or let-
ting the pregnant mother hamster out of her cage during
recess so her babies were born on a stack of yellow construction paper in the back of the supply closet. That sort
of thing. Nothing bad enough to go to jail, but I couldn't
help myself. School made me crazy.

"It's not that you're *bad*, Benjamin," my mother would
tell me. "In fact, your reading is so much better and your
eye-hand coordination is improving and even your lisp."
My mother sounds out the word "lisp" every time she says
it as if it's a word with three syllables: *li—ssss—ppp*.

It drives me wild.

"Every teacher is mad at me before she even meets
me," I would say.

"You just have a bad reputation, which started with
the teddy bear, and now you can't control yourself," my
mother replied. "The teachers expect you'll be a problem,
so it's up to you to change their minds."

It wasn't entirely because of the teddy bear, although I
hold Mary Sue Briggs responsible for every bad thing in
my life, including the viral pneumonia I caught from her
last year. But my bad reputation has followed me like a tail
getting longer every year.

Every September, I go to a new grade and have a new
teacher, new school clothes, new books and pencils and
erasers, and think to myself that this year everything will

be different. The teacher will *like* me and she'll tell the other teachers what a terrific kid I am in spite of my old reputation. She'll even tell Mr. O'Dell. But *no*. On the first day of school in September, the teacher stands at the front of the room and reads the roll and asks us to raise our hands when our name is called so she can identify us. And when she comes to my name, "Benjamin A. Carter"—A for Anthony, a name I hate—she stops and looks around the room and shakes her head as if a black X is spilled over my name. Somehow like magic, as if I give off a certain bad cheesy smell, things fall apart when I walk into a room at school. Only at school. Everyplace else, like home and my grandparents' and birthday parties and after-school soccer when I don't have some stupid special tutor trying to fix my learning disabilities, I'm fine. I mean, almost fine. I'm not exactly a perfect child, but I'm not a criminal either.

But at school I'm a disaster. I walk into a room, like, say, Mr. Eager's third grade, and a bookcase falls over; Billy Bass tips his chair backwards, hits his head on the floor, and gets a concussion; Patricia Dale trips over my foot in music class and knocks out her front tooth and tells *everyone* I did it on purpose.

People just expect things to go wrong when I'm around. And they do.

* * *

"I think you're uncomfortable at school," Meg said to me one afternoon last year.

"How come?"

"Because you're just a little different, not entirely a middle-of-the-road, regular ten-year-old boy."

"Because of the lisp?"

"I think it *started* with the lisp," Meg said. "Everybody at home thought you were funny and adorable saying things like 'thweetheart,' and then you went to school and you weren't funny any longer. You were *wrong*. Other kids didn't talk like you did."

"Well, Daniel Forest had a lisp."

"And then he moved to New York."

"My teachers say I try to call attention to myself by bad behavior. They say my lisp is just an excuse and sometimes I do it on purpose just to call attention to myself."

Meg shrugged. "The thing is, if people expect you to be trouble, then you'll be trouble. People expect me to be good, so I'm good. It's the way people are."

"Stupid."

"Right. Stupid," Meg said.

Which is just one of the reasons Meg is my best friend.

That night when I went to bed, I thought about what Meg had said, because she's smart in school but she's especially smart about kids. I thought about the word "uncomfortable" and just thinking about it, I felt a little sick. When

I'm at school, it's as if my skin is squishing me like too-tight jeans. I have this funny feeling in my stomach and I can't sit still at my desk, and sometimes I think kids are looking at me like I'm weird.

Every day since the Halloween when Mary Sue Briggs made fun of me, I've gone up the front steps of Stockton Elementary with that same feeling in my stomach. Because of my lisp, like Meg says. Because of my *special* teachers and my learning disabilities. Because everyone—first the teachers and then the kids—is looking at me waiting to see what will happen next.

And then the week after Easter break, fifth grade, section number three, Mr. Baker's class, Trout arrived. He walked into the classroom wearing jeans and a white T-shirt with his name on the front in black letters and carrying a book bag.

"I'm Trout," he said to Mr. Baker.

"I know," Mr. Baker said. "Welcome to the fifth grade. I've kept a desk for you right here in the front row."

But Trout wasn't paying attention to Mr. Baker. He took one look around the classroom, considering the possibilities for a friend, and decided on me.

And that was that. When the bell rang for the end of homeroom, he jumped up from his chair, rushed over three rows to where I was sitting, and attached himself like Velcro to my side.

CHAPTER THREE

Trout is tall, almost as tall as my father, and skinny, with soft yellow hair that hangs below his ears and glasses and a deep dimple in his chin. I wouldn't have noticed the dimple if he hadn't drawn a question mark in the middle of it with bright red Magic Marker. Really red, like a tomato. The question mark started just below his lip, filled the space of his chin with its reverse C and short line at the bottom with a dot at the very tip. A perfect question mark. I couldn't take my eyes off it.

"I hate this school," Trout said to me after first period when I was walking with him to the library to meet Ms. Bissell.

"Yeah," I said, half agreeing with him, which I did.

"I could tell I'd hate it here the minute I got here. This school has a kind of bad smell," Trout said.

He was sauntering along beside me. He walked with his body sort of sloped, his long legs stretching out in front of him like a runner in slow motion, a confident walk. He was a confident kid, or so I thought, interested in him from the start in spite of what my father would call "my better judgment." I mean anyone with a question mark on his chin can't be very worried about what people think. Right?

"A bad smell?" I sniffed.

It smelled like a perfectly ordinary school to me, the same as it always smelled.

"I've been here since first grade and this is how Stockton Elementary smells," I said.

"Well, I'm going to change that," Trout said.

"Yeah," I said.

I had to say something, but as we walked into the library and Ms. Bissell looked up from her papers to give me a little wave, I wondered how you change the smell of a place as big as a school.

My mother sprays this pine-smelling stuff if Jetty pees on the rug. But a whole school? And did Stockton Elementary have a particular smell that I'd been missing all these years?

Ms. Bissell is older than the rest of the teachers at Stockton, and we're a little afraid of her. You get the sense that noise, even the slightest noise, upsets her. Not that she'd lose her temper or shout or send one of us to Mr. O'Dell's office. Instead, she might put her head down on the desk and sob. That's my mother's word for a lot of crying, which I don't do, and neither does Meg, but Belinda, on the second floor of our apartment building, sobs all the time.

"Trout?" Ms. Bissell said. "That's a very interesting name. Mr. Baker said you'd be coming to check out the library."

"Yeah," Trout said.

"And Trout is your first name?"

"First and last name," Trout said.

"Trout Trout," Ms. Bissell said thoughtfully.

"That's right. Trout Trout," he enunciated. "I don't have a middle name."

"So, Trout," Ms. Bissell said softly. "Welcome to the Stockton Elementary library." She was very proud of the library, as you can tell from the way she calls it by name. "Do you enjoy reading?" she asked.

"We don't have books at our house. We keep moving every few months or so and my father says we can only move the necessities." He picked up a copy of *To Kill a Mockingbird*, which was in the OUT box on Ms. Bissell's desk.

"Have you read *To Kill a Mockingbird?*" she asked. "It's one of my favorites."

Trout shook his head.

"I don't read," he said.

"You don't *like* to read?" Ms. Bissell asked. Her voice was kind, not critical, just inquiring, but I could feel Trout stiffen next to me, move away from her desk, fold his arms across his chest.

"I don't like to read. We didn't have to read books in my old school."

"Which was in Georgia?"

"I lived in Georgia until yesterday," Trout said, "but before Georgia we lived in Kansas, and before that, Mississippi, and before that, Florida. I'm really from the world."

He has a kind of "don't mess around with me" voice, with a "one step closer to where I'm standing and you're history" sound to it. Sort of a tough guy, but I could tell he wasn't *really* a tough guy. I don't know how I can tell those things about a person, but I can.

"That's very interesting," Ms. Bissell said. "Perhaps you'll tell us something about the places you've lived. For example, I've never been to Mississippi."

Trout shrugged.

"It must be very hot in the summer."

But Trout seemed to have finished talking. He jabbed me in the shoulder and nodded his head in the direction of the door.

"Hot as hell," he said to Ms. Bissell.

Ms. Bissell stood up a little straighter, leaned forward across the desk, her hands flat on the table.

"In my library class, Trout," she began, and the veins in her neck were standing out like small blue pipes, "you don't use swear words and you can't wear a red question mark on your chin."

Her voice was very quiet. I almost had to strain to hear, but I knew that voice from third grade when I was a problem in library class and she had asked me to leave and not return until the next year.

"Benjamin," she had said, bringing me up to her desk so the other kids couldn't hear what she was saying, "get your books and leave and don't return until next September."

And that was that.

"The question mark is permanent," Trout was saying. "It's a permanent tattoo."

"It doesn't matter what it is. You won't be wearing it in my class," Ms. Bissell said.

"S'okay," Trout said, putting *To Kill a Mockingbird* back in Ms. Bissell's OUT box and leading me out of the library.

Ms. Bissell had already returned to her papers and didn't look up as we left, although I waved to her and said goodbye and that I'd see her later, hoping she wouldn't hold Trout's comments against me.

I was already headed down the corridor before I realized I had left Trout behind. When I looked back, he was standing in the open door to the library fiddling with something in his hand, so I headed back in his direction, and just then I smelled the most terrible smell I've ever known, like a hundred dogs the size of Jetty were using the library as a dumping ground.

"Let's get out of here before that stupid librarian sees us."

I was holding my nose.

"Don't you smell that?" I asked. I should have known better than to ask.

"Smell?"

We were rushing down the corridor and he was laughing so hard he could hardly stand up.

"It's like, I don't know, the worst smell . . ."

Behind us we could hear the other kids making choking sounds as the smell spread down the corridor.

I looked at Trout. "Did you make that happen?"

"I told you I didn't like the smell of this school," he said.

I ducked into the boys' room after him.

"Want to see?" he asked, reaching in his pocket and putting out his hand. In the palm of his hand was a little brown pill about the size of the vitamin C I have to take to keep from getting colds.

"What's that?" I asked.

"Fart Fun," Trout said. "Keep it. You may need it some-time."

He put the pill in my hand.

"You open the capsule and out comes this smell called Fart Fun. That's the name of the pill. I've got hundreds at home I got at a magic store in Georgia. I always carry some in my pocket."

"So that's why you asked about the smell of the school, right?"

"Right. I thought the school needed smell improve-ment and, presto, I had just the stuff."

When we came out of the bathroom, the bell was ringing for the next period and the smell had almost disappeared.

"It doesn't last," Trout said.

"You're not afraid of getting caught?"

"I've never been caught."

"Cool," I said, and I meant it. I'd never known anyone at Stockton Elementary who wasn't scared of trouble, and Trout didn't seem to be worried at all.

"So?" Trout said as we walked into homeroom. "I sup-pose you're wondering where I got the question mark on my chin."

From a distance, it looked like a bright red sunburn or an infected mosquito bite. Or a big zit. Close up, it looked like what it was. A question mark very neatly made.

"I always wear a question mark on my chin. I had it tattooed when I was six at a place in Florida where they burn the tattoo into your skin too deep to ever come off," he said.

"Didn't it hurt?" I asked, amazed that a boy my age would be allowed to have a tattoo. Max has a tattoo, a lizard or an iguana, some kind of cold-blooded creature tattooed on his shoulder. He decided to show it to me over Christmas vacation.

But Max is a senior in high school, grown-up enough to pay for his own tattoo.

"Did it hurt?"

Trout looked at me as if I'd lost my brains.

"I mean it must've, right?"

"Of course it hurt," he said. "It killed."

"Then why did you do it?" I asked.

Trout shrugged as if my question were too foolish to answer.

"I suppose you're wondering what it means. Everybody asks me how come I have a question mark instead of like a flower or a knife or some kind of dog or cat or stupid bird."

I nodded, although I was still thinking about Fart Fun and hadn't gotten around to wondering what the question mark meant. It didn't even occur to me that a question mark would mean something.

"So guess," Trout said.

"I can't. I'm a bad guesser anyway," I said. "Just tell me what it means."

"It means, who knows what's going to happen with me around. I'm a big question mark," he said, shoving my shoulder in a friendly way. "Get it?"

"Right," I said. "I get it."

He gave me a funny look. "Do you really get it?"

"Sort of," I said, which was a lie.

The bell was ringing for recess and it was raining, which meant that recess would be in the gym, so I told Trout to come along with me and he could meet some of the kids in the class, since he'd only been at Stockton Elementary for a couple of hours.

"Did you have a lot of friends in Georgia?" I asked Trout as we headed to the gym for recess.

"Not a lot," he said. "Hardly any except a girl named Josie, who smoked. But we move so much I don't have time to make friends."

"And will you be moving from Stockton soon?" I asked.

He shrugged. "I never know."

"I bet kids remember you after you move even if you didn't get to know them," I said, taking a sideways look at his face. But from the right side, it was difficult to get the full picture of his chin.

"How come?"

"Because of the question mark, dummy," I said. "I don't think a lot of kids have one of those. At least none I know. None I've ever known."

Trout gave me a funny look, his eyebrows high on his forehead, his lips a little wrinkly, as if he were trying to decide what to say.

"You know what?" He began watching me carefully, for my reaction, I guess.

I shook my head. "I don't know," I said. "Tell me what."

"If I didn't have a question mark on my chin, I'd be invisible," Trout said. "No one would even know I was here."

CHAPTER FOUR

"Invisible" is a word I've thought about a lot. It's something I'd like to be, especially at school. Especially last year in the fifth grade, and the year before, and the year before that, since I have such a bad reputation. Anytime something happens in my presence, I'm the one blamed for trouble. So it'd be great not to be seen at all.

"Ben? Absent again," the teacher would say during roll call.

"Yup," the class would say. "Absent again."

And there I'd be, sitting at my desk chewing bubble gum, sticking it on the bottom of the chair, my feet up on the desk, my baseball cap on backwards.

But no one would know. I'd be able to see everyone perfectly, but they couldn't see me when I stuck my foot into the aisle, and Ms. Percival tripped on it and knocked out her front teeth, so she had to have fake ones.

Invisible, I'd simply walk into homeroom and stand on my head and dump Mary Sue Briggs out of her chair and throw a few water balloons, maybe one just over the teacher's desk, splashing water all over his grade book. Then I'd jump on top of the desk and do a dance, knocking the spelling tests on the floor, kicking the tulip pot so the dirt spread over the social studies projects.

"What's going on?" the teacher would shout as everything was flying off his desk. "This is crazy." He'd scramble on the floor picking up the spelling papers. "Something insane is going on here."

But of course the teacher couldn't see me, so what could he do? I'd take the sports jacket off the back of his chair, put it on, and race around the classroom. The only thing anyone could see would be a sports jacket sailing around the room all by itself.

Invisible sounds swell and I told Trout.

We were walking back into the classroom after recess, standing at my locker while I got my math book.

"I'd like to be invisible sometimes," I said. "It sounds cool."

He shrugged. He was rummaging in his book bag for something and took out a long silver tube like toothpaste with a black X on it.

"Invisible cream," he said. "Try it."

I looked at the tube, which was half empty, took off the top, and smelled it. It had a kind of sharp, acid smell and the cream was pale pink.

"What does it do?"

"Try it."

"Not unless you tell me what will happen."

"Like if you put it on your eyebrows, your eyebrows will disappear."

"Forever?"

"Until you wash it off. Here." He took the tube and squeezed it into his hand and rubbed a little on my forehead. "Go check the mirror in the boys' room."

I got the rest of my books and headed to the boys' room, Trout on my heels. The bathroom was very bright, but I couldn't see anything on my forehead when I looked in the mirror, not even the faintest pink.

"It didn't work," I said.

"Wait."

"Now? Don't we have to go to class?"

"Just wait and maybe your forehead will disappear. Or maybe you're just not the invisible kind of kid."

So we went to math and I had forgotten the invisible cream by the time my math test was handed back with a fifty-six in red across the top and a note at the bottom from Ms. Becker: "Dear Ben, Do you *ever* do your homework or study for tests?"

"Ben?" Ms. Becker called out.

And I was just thinking, Great, now she's going to call me to the front of the class and tell everyone I got a fifty-six *again* and didn't try and wasn't smart, so I looked up at her and her face turned something like purple. She's old, and purple isn't a good color for her.

"What?" I said, forgetting to be polite. And what good would it have done anyway?

"What is on your forehead?"

I looked over, and Trout had an expression of boredom on his face.

"I don't know," I said.

"Certainly you know. You put it there to be amusing, I'm sure, and distract the class."

I reached up and touched my forehead. It was kind of hot and burning, but I hadn't noticed. By this time the class had jumped out of their seats in spite of Ms. Becker and run up to the front of the class to look at me. Ms. Becker asked everyone to sit down, which they didn't, and to stop laughing, which they didn't, and I was sent to Mr. O'Dell's office.

I went. In fact, I was glad to get away from Ms. Becker and have a chance to tear up my math test and toss it in the trash in the boys' room, where I went first to check what had happened to my forehead.

Across my forehead, in bright red letters, was written ASS.

"So thanks a lot," I said to Trout.

"I'm really sorry," Trout said sweetly. "I didn't know she'd be so mean. What happened in the principal's office?"

"I washed it off before I got to the principal's office and told him my sister's boyfriend had given me some magic cream and I used it on my forehead without knowing what it would do and how stupid that was and how sorry I was," I said. "That kind of stuff. I go to Mr. O'Dell's office so much I've learned how to suck up and he's pretty dumb."

"Are we still going to be best friends?"

"We were never going to be best friends," I said. We were headed out of the building on our way to meet Meg, which had been my plan before Trout arrived at Stockton Elementary.

"Then friends?"

"Maybe," I said. But already Trout was the most interesting boy I'd met since I came to Stockton when I was five years old, so it was pretty much sealed that we were going to be friends.

Usually Meg walks home from the high school by Main Street, stopping at the pharmacy to see our mother, who'll be standing behind the counter mixing up pills, and sometimes at The Grub, where the high school kids go after school to smoke and drink Coke floats and hang out and play music. Often I go to The Grub with Meg as sort of a pet. That's how her friends think of me. Toy baby brother. Pet brother. I don't mind it.

Max is always outside The Grub leaning against the wall of the brick building, listening to the music coming through the window, smoking with some of his friends.

So on Trout's first day of school I took him to The Grub with me. I really didn't have a choice. Already he was attached. I couldn't strip myself away.

"Are we going to your house?" he asked as we headed down the front steps of the school.

"We're meeting my older sister at a place called The Grub," I said.

"Do you drink?" Trout asked, falling in step with me.

"Nope."

"Do they serve beer at The Grub?"

"Just hamburgers, Cokes, that sort of thing," I told him. "The kids who go are underage. You know. They can't buy alcohol."

He seemed disappointed.

He was walking along beside me, his hands slipped into the pockets of his jeans, the sleeves of his sweatshirt rolled up, when he asked me about pills.

"Pills?"

"Yeah, pills."

"You mean like drugs?"

"Yeah, drugs. But not street drugs. These are the kinds of drugs you get from the doctor for dumb and dumber kids who're in trouble in school."

"Well, I should be taking those pills," I said, walking down Main Street in the direction of The Grub. "I'm always in trouble."

"For bad grades?"

"Bad grades, bad behavior, you name it."

"I get in a lot of trouble too," Trout said.

I wasn't surprised. Anyone could tell that Trout was that kind of kid.

"I'm supposed to take Ritalin. That's what the doctor in Kansas gave me to take in third grade," he said. "You know about Ritalin?"

"I've heard of it."

"Well, it's a pill."

I knew all about Ritalin. When I was told I had learning disabilities, Mr. O'Dell told my parents that *everyone* thought I should take Ritalin and my mother said no, I would not be taking Ritalin or anything else. She was a pharmacist and knew all about pills and I was her son and she would be making her own decisions about me. My mom can't be pushed around, especially about her kids.

"So what's Ritalin?" I had asked my mom on the drive home from O'Dell's office.

"Medicine to make you calm down so you can study," my mother said. "And that's something you're going to learn how to do without medicine."

The subject of Ritalin came up again in fifth grade and my mom hadn't changed her mind. But so far, even now, I haven't learned how to calm down and study. At least according to my teachers.

"I'm supposed to take Ritalin so I can concentrate in school, whatever that means," Trout said. "The teachers in Kansas said I had to take the stuff because I was a 'cutup' with learning disabilities."

"Learning disabilities?" My heart leapt up.

"Yeah. Dyslexia," Trout said. "You know dyslexia?"

"I've heard of it."

I knew dyslexia very well. It's one of the things that's supposed to be the matter with me. I reverse my letters and can't write very quickly and am especially slow on the standardized reading tests, which I hate.

"How did the teachers know you had learning disabilities?" I asked.

I wasn't planning to tell Trout about my own learning disabilities, but I had this sudden feeling of lightness just to know that he had the same troubles I do. Sometimes at Stockton Elementary, I've felt completely alone, even by the time I got to fifth grade and my lisp had almost disappeared.

"I couldn't read," he said. "I still can't, and don't even want to read most of the time, since school is so boring. But that's why they gave me Ritalin, so I could learn to read."

"Does it help?"

"Who knows?" Trout shrugged. "I throw the pills in the toilet."

I laughed. I couldn't help myself.

"And what does your father say about that?"

He looked at me with exasperation.

"He doesn't know, of course. If he knew, he'd tie me to a chair and stick the pills down my throat." He opened his mouth, gagging, stuck his finger down his throat. "Like that," he said.

We turned into The Grub. I knew Trout was impressed when I just breezed past the high school boys leaning, as they always did, against the brick building. I high-fived Max, opened the door of The Grub, and walked in as if I owned the place. A bunch of kids were waving to me, calling me by name. "Benjamin!" they shouted. "Hey, Benjamin." That's what Meg calls me. But I'm Ben to my friends.

"So, buddy," Max said to Trout as we walked by him. "What're you doing with that splotch on your chin? Gangrene?"

"Can't you tell a question mark when you see one?"

Max laughed. "A question mark. Very funny. I like that. So you got a tattoo and you're still a baby."

"Right. A tattoo at six, buddy," Trout said.

We had Cokes and hung around Meg and her friends, and Trout loved it since Meg's friend Shoshanna leaned her elbow on his shoulder and ran her fingers through his thin, silky hair. He kind of wiggled, embarrassed at first, and then he got a funny smile spreading all over his face.

"You are beyond rad," Shoshanna said, pulling his hair. "What'd you say your name is?"

"Trout."

"Trout. That's a funny name. What's your last name?"

"Trout." They both laughed then and Shoshanna gave him a huge hug.

"You are beyond cool, Trout Trout. Beyond heart-break."

"Knock it off, Shoshanna," Meg said.

"He loves it," Shoshanna said. "Don'tcha, Trout Trout?"

Trout shrugged.

Later Trout told me that he thought Shoshanna was a maniac. His words. And wasn't it amazing, he asked me, that a fifteen-year-old girl, even a dumb and crazy one like Shoshanna, thought he was good-looking?

But later Meg told me that she hated what Shoshanna had done by teasing Trout, since anyone with sense ought to have noticed that a boy like Trout with a question mark on his chin had problems.

"What kind of problems do you think he has?" I asked, walking home with her after Trout had left for home. "I mean, he's got learning disabilities, but so do I."

"Who *doesn't* have learning disabilities?"

"You don't," I said. "You were born smart."

Which is when I told her about invisible. Not the invisible cream, but what Trout said about being invisible.

Meg thinks a lot. That's something I like about her. She doesn't say things "off the top of her head," as my mother would say, meaning that Meg thinks before she speaks. So I knew that she'd have something important to say about invisible.

We were on Acorn Road, where Ms. Percival lives with her mother, Mrs. Percival, in a dark brown house. I like to walk fast on Acorn, hoping not to see Ms. Percival. I don't care about seeing her mother.

Meg was quiet for a while. She and Max had had a fight. Max had asked was she going with him to the Spring Dance and she said no, she wasn't going to the Spring Dance unless he stopped smoking, and he said, "Eat your heart out, Megsie." She threw her arm around my shoulder and walked away, telling Max she'd never speak to him again. She's said that to Max quite a few times and

I keep hoping she'll keep her promise, but she always forgets.

So it was just the two of us hunched together under her green crocodile umbrella, our bodies bumping into each other in that way I love, as if it's just us alone in the world together and we're best friends and we'll never get any older than we are now.

"So tell me what Trout said about invisible."

I repeated what I remembered.

" 'If I didn't have a question mark on my chin,' Trout said, 'I'd be invisible. No one would even know that I was here.' " I looked up at her. "Like that."

Meg looked thoughtful.

"I think invisible would be fun," I said.

But she was thinking. I knew better than to keep talking while she was thinking, so we just walked along Tabor Lane, down Arch Street behind the movie theater and the ice cream store, across Bark, down the alley that's behind our apartment building, and in the back door.

Belinda was sitting on the stoop behind the apartment, pulling double bubble gum in a long string from her mouth. She took it out as we walked by and stuck her tongue out at me.

That's the kind of relationship I have with Belinda. Megan too. Which is why the only friend I have in the apartment building is Meg.

Meg and I got the mail in the entry hall and walked up the steps, and it wasn't until we got into the apartment itself and Meg was taking out the package of chocolate chip cookies and gallon of milk she'd gotten at the market that she spoke.

"I think Trout must be miserable."

"You think so?"

"Imagine feeling invisible," she said, pouring us both a glass of milk, tearing open the package of cookies.

"I did imagine. It felt great. Invisible, I could get away with anything."

"Maybe for you," Meg said, sitting at the kitchen table. "I don't think it feels that way to Trout."

"How come?" I asked.

"If you're invisible, then no one knows you're there. Isn't that right?"

"Right."

"Which means you don't matter because you don't exist."

"I didn't think of it that way," I said.

"But I bet Trout does. I bet that's why he has a question mark on his chin. At least if people don't see him, they see the question mark."

"Yeah," I said. "I guess that's true."

And I knew Meg was probably right about Trout. She is always right about people, especially kids.

CHAPTER FIVE

When I got to school the next morning, Trout was waiting for me. I was late because it was raining and I had left my math homework on the kitchen table, so I went back to the apartment, and when I got there, the dog had peed on my mother's favorite rug in the living room. First I had to clean that up and take the dog out and put him in the kitchen so he wouldn't do it again. By the time I got to school, the second bell had rung. Homeroom was under way and Trout was standing in the rain on the bottom step of the school.

"Hi," he said. "I was afraid maybe you were going to be absent."

"Nope. I'm never absent," I said. "But you shouldn't wait. You get in trouble if you're late."

"No problem," Trout said, taking the steps two at a time.

He stood beside me while I put my books away in my locker. He had a way of standing very close so I could almost feel his breath on my neck, as if he were afraid I might escape. It drove me crazy, but in a funny kind of way I didn't mind. No one had ever liked me so much and so quickly.

"So what're we doing this afternoon?" he was asking.

"I have an appointment," I said.

"Doctor's?" he asked.

The fact is, I had tutoring in reading as usual, but I wasn't ready to let Trout know. Not yet, at least.

"Nope," I said, and then, realizing I had to give an answer, I told him I had an appointment with the dentist.

I was rearranging the books in my locker, getting my social studies book out of my backpack, looking for my library book, and when I stood up and turned around to face Trout, I noticed something different about his chin.

"So what're you looking at?" he asked.

What I had noticed was that the ink of his tattoo was running in a thin red line down his chin, falling onto the front of his shirt.

"Is something wrong?" he asked.

"I don't know," I said, heading for the classroom, Trout right beside me. "It looks a little like your tattoo is melting."

He reached up and touched his chin, took his hand, now smudged red, away from his face and looked at it.

"Jeez." He wiped the red on his jeans. "I'm going to the bathroom and see what's going on."

I was at my desk getting ready for social studies when Trout came back, checked in with Mr. Baker, and passed by my desk, which is at the front of the room, leaning his chin towards me so I could check out the question mark.

"So?"

"Looks okay to me," I said.

"You were right," he said. "It was melting."

Later I wondered how a tattoo could melt. I don't know very much about tattoos. Most of Meg's friends have tattoos, flowers on their backs or little snakes crawling up their legs, dumb things to get painted on yourself for the rest of your life, my mother said. So Meg isn't allowed to have a tattoo and wouldn't get one anyway. She thinks for herself, like I said. What I know is that a tattoo is made by sticking needles with dye in your skin, so your skin is actually colored forever and should never melt.

I wouldn't want to do something on purpose that hurts. And needles hurt. So I sat in homeroom imagining what it must have felt like for Trout when he was six years old to have this red question mark made from needles on his chin.

When the bell rang for social studies, Trout was beside me, fiddling with his chin as if he were afraid the whole question mark was going to fall off on the floor.

Next we went to Spanish and math and language arts and lunch and gym and visual arts and community service. In each class, he sat at the desk beside me, slid halfway down the wooden chair so it looked as if he was going to fall on the floor, and looked at the teacher through half-closed lizard eyes.

"Hello, Trout," each teacher would begin at the start of class. "And what's your last name? Even though it's your second day at Stockton, your name hasn't been added to our roll lists yet."

"O'Donnell," Trout said in Spanish class.

"Barrigan," he said in math.

"Jobman," he said in language arts.

"Harper," he said in community service.

No one contradicted him, but by the time we got to gym, where he said his last name was Raven, we were struggling not to laugh.

"How come you change your name all the time?" I asked after gym.

"I get bored easily," Trout said.

"So what's your real last name?" I asked.

"Benefit," he said.

But it wasn't Benefit either. And not Trout. I found that out at the end of school that day when Mr. Baker said goodbye.

"Sanger, right?" Mr. Baker asked. "Your papers were finally sent down from the office. Morris Sanger, nickname Trout." Trout considered for a moment, but he left the classroom without answering.

"So is Mr. Baker right?" I asked when I got to my locker, where he was waiting.

"Trout is my name."

"No last name?"

"No."

"Cool," I said. But there was something in the tense way he held his body that made me nervous, as if at any moment he might slam his fist into a wall.

"So I'll go to the dentist with you and then we can go back to your apartment," he said.

It had stopped raining, but the streets were wet, and we slopped through the muddy sidewalks headed away from Stockton Elementary. I was on my way to tutoring in a building behind my mother's pharmacy, where all the kids who have to be tutored in Stockton, New Jersey, go after school. It's call the Reading and Math Center and I usually slink in the back door and up the steps to Ms. Sutton's office so no one will see me. I certainly wasn't planning to take Trout along.

"You can meet me at my apartment in about an hour," I said.

"What about the dentist?"

"I go to the dentist alone."

I gave him directions to my apartment.

"Just wait outside," I said, and headed off to tutoring.

And he did.

There he was when I got back from tutoring, sitting on the top step of our building looking for me.

He followed me into the building and asked could he stay for dinner.

I didn't know what to say. It was after five o'clock and my mother's night to cook, and she'd probably gotten just enough food for four on her way home. We shop every day for dinner just in case we decide at the last minute that we want a pizza or to go to the movies and eat popcorn instead of dinner or to go to my grandparents' in the next town. Every day is different in our house. We make last-minute decisions and change plans and have picnics by the Stockton lake when the day is particularly warm and ice cream sundaes at Lotsa Love Shoppe on Main Street for dinner. Most of my friends eat dinner at six-thirty and then homework and then TV and then bed. Our life is nothing like that.

"So what do you think?" Trout asked as I opened the door to our apartment.

"About dinner?" I asked. "Sure, why not."

We hung out and played Cringe. Belinda came over with some chocolate chip cookie dough, which she shared with us—they never get to baking the cookies at Belinda's house, only making the dough. Belinda put on my mother's high-heeled shoes and a red beret and a ski parka, and sat on our couch staring at Trout's chin. Although it was a warm spring day, she seemed happy in winter clothes watching us play Cringe.

Cringe is a game that my father made up when I was having the worst trouble in school. We made the whole game working in the back of his hardware store. For a couple of years we played most nights, my treat after I finished my homework.

The Cringe board is like a checkerboard except yellow and black. There is a stack of cards and each player gets fifteen cards, some blank and some with a figure of a creep on the front. There's the Bully with the head of a bull and the body of a wimp, and the Brains with an enormous head spilling yucky green stuff all over the card, and the Tease, which is a girl octopus—curly hair, ribbons, that sort of stuff—with a tiny knife clutched in each one of her tentacles. The object of the game is to get rid of the creeps and end up with a hand of blank cards. The person with the most blanks wins. It's my favorite game, and for the worst years at Stockton Elementary, when I failed everything and was always in trouble, playing Cringe was the only thing that made me happy.

"So we're friends, right?" Trout asked after the first game of Cringe, which I won. "Real friends, right?"

"Right," I said.

"Are you guys best friends?" Belinda asked, climbing down from the couch.

"He's my best friend," Trout said. "We're kind of matching kids, don'tcha think, Ben?"

I shrugged. "Except for the invisible cream."

"But you're not still mad at me, are you? I didn't mean to do anything bad to you."

I didn't say anything. I liked Trout and of course I feel important when someone likes me a lot. But I didn't want him to be my best friend. Not yet.

"Dunno," I replied.

"Well, I don't think you should be best friends with Ben," Belinda said to Trout.

She took off the beret and my mother's high heels, put her hands on her hips, and told Trout she thought he was weird.

"*Weird*," she said again, and took her bowl of cookie dough, walked across the living room and out the door, leaving my mother's high heels in the middle of the room.

I would have made her put the shoes back except the telephone was ringing, and when I answered, it was Mr.

Baker, and when I told him she was still at work, he said he'd call back. He didn't sound happy.

I hate it when teachers call our house. It's never about something good. And every year, sometimes every month or so, my teacher calls to talk to my mom about something I'm doing wrong. I wish my mom understood how much I try to be good and it never works. Even with Mr. Baker.

So I was surprised and worried about Mr. Baker calling. Not that he likes me. But he doesn't dislike me as much as some of the other teachers I've had. I don't drive him crazy, at least.

Trout left after dinner. My mother cooked halibut and split it five ways and gave Trout her piece of blueberry pie and then drove him to his house because it was dark.

"He's an odd boy, isn't he?" she said when she got back and Meg and I were finishing the dishes.

"You mean he's odd because of the question-mark thing?" I asked.

My mother sat down at the kitchen table.

"Well."

"It's a tattoo he got when he was six," I said. "He probably didn't know any better."

"He got a tattoo so he wouldn't feel invisible," Meg said.

"So he told me," my mother said. "He didn't mention

53

invisible but he told me about getting the question mark burned on his skin."

"Yeah, me too," I said.

"It's not a tattoo," my mother said.

"Did he tell you that?" Meg asked.

"No, he told me it *was* one."

"So?" I said, suddenly protective of Trout. I don't know what happened to me because usually I don't argue with my mother. But suddenly I wanted to tell her that Trout was my best friend and she better be nice to him, better believe what he told her.

"It isn't a tattoo," my mother said quietly.

"How do you know?" Meg asked.

"Because it weeps."

"Weeps?" That was me speaking.

"I was looking at his face as he got out of the car and the red ink from the question mark was dripping down his chin. A tattoo doesn't do that."

I didn't bother to tell her that I'd seen the same thing, that I'd wondered about a dripping tattoo as well. I wasn't going to betray my friend, even with my mother, and I didn't like to hear that my mother, of all people, doubted him. I didn't like that at all.

"What if he *wants* you to think it's a tattoo?" Meg asked. "What if that's important to him?"

"I was concerned that he felt the need to lie," my mother said.

My mother is like that, worried about right and wrong all the time, which drives me crazy. Because as far as I can tell from eleven years on the planet, what feels like right is sometimes wrong and what feels wrong is sometimes right.

But that's another subject we'll get into later in this story.

"I lie to you, Mom. I need to lie two or three times a day," Meg said. " 'Why were you late for dinner tonight?' you asked me. 'I was at the dry cleaners picking up your clothes,' I answered. But that wasn't true. I was actually at Viv's house and only picked up the dry cleaning at the last minute. I tell that kind of lie all the time."

The telephone rang just as my mom was about to lose her temper at Meg, which she sometimes does and it makes her face go red as cranberries and her top lip quivers. It was Mr. Baker.

"Oh, hello, Mr. Baker," Mom said. "I'm so glad you called."

So I went into my room and Meg turned on her music quite loud so I couldn't possibly hear my mother's end of the conversation, which went on and on and on. All I could do was watch through a crack in my bedroom door as my mom paced the living room, mostly listening to Mr. Baker on the other end of the phone. Finally I checked Meg's room and she was painting her fingernails purple and didn't want to talk, so I climbed into my bed and waited.

That's when my mother came in.

"Mr. Baker has been pleased with you recently," she said.

"Yeah."

"He says your attitude is better. Not great but better. He says you're becoming more of a citizen."

"What's that?"

"Just a good guy."

I could tell bad news was coming. Good news first to soften me up, and then slammo, the bad news explodes.

I sat up against my headboard.

"What else?" I asked.

"Well, Mr. Baker is worried about Trout."

I shrugged.

"Why doesn't he call Trout's father?" I said. "Not you."

"Because he's worried about the effect Trout could have on *you*," she said in that way she has, her voice soft enough, almost friendly. But that doesn't mean she'll put up with disagreement from me.

"Like what effect?"

"Like getting in more trouble instead of less."

So there you have it. "The Trout Problem." Before the end of fifth grade, "The Trout Problem" got so awful I was forced to do something surprising, something I can't believe I had the courage to do, even now, a year later, with Trout gone.

CHAPTER SIX

The next morning Trout called me with a plan. He called very early, even before I went in the kitchen for breakfast, and told me he'd already left his house and was calling from a phone booth. He wanted to meet me outside school at eight o'clock.

"What's the plan?" I asked, still in my pajamas.

"It's going to be really funny," he said.

"Like how funny?" I asked.

"I can't tell you now," he said. "Just meet me on the blacktop behind the school."

So I got dressed in a hurry, brushed my teeth, and went downstairs for breakfast with my book bag already packed and ready to go.

"Why so early?" my mother asked. She was suspicious, I could tell. She worries about me, not that anything bad will happen to me but that I'll cause trouble. Every afternoon—this is what Meg told me—she's afraid some teacher is going to call the pharmacy to tell her more bad news about me, like Ms. Becker did when the invisible cream turned into ASS.

"Where did you get that cream?" my mother had asked that evening. "Max?"

I didn't answer. I wasn't going to tell her Trout had given it to me and I'd already told Mr. O'Dell about Max, so I said nothing at all, and by the next day, my mom sort of forgot it. But she did say, because she worries all the time, "You should never put anything on your face unless you know what it is. It could've been poison."

"It's not *so* early to go to school," I said. "I just promised to meet some guys from fifth grade on the blacktop behind school."

I poured milk on my cereal and pretended to be interested in eating, which I wasn't. I only wanted to get out of the house and meet Trout and find out about his plan.

"Benjamin." My mother sat down at the table beside me, speaking quietly so Meg, who was making toast, wouldn't hear what she was saying, even though I tell Meg everything. "Are you leaving early to meet Trout?" she asked.

I considered lying. I thought I could name a few guys in my class who I might be meeting before school, but my mother seems to know what I'm thinking about even when I don't say it. It's as if she can see straight through the skin and bone to my brain. So I didn't make up a story. I mean, I didn't lie exactly, but I didn't tell "the whole truth and nothing but the truth," as my father would say.

"I'm helping Trout with his math homework," I said, finishing my cereal, dumping the extra milk in the sink.

"I see." My mother gave me one of her looks.

I could have said, "I can tell you don't believe me," or "I'm almost telling the truth," or I could have said, "I'm meeting Trout Trout on the blacktop and we're going to make plans to get kicked out of school," but instead I followed Meg out the front door and down the back stairs.

"What was *that* all about?" she asked.

I shrugged. "Mom didn't believe I was going to be helping Trout with his math homework."

"She's right," Meg said. "You're flunking math." My sister is straightforward and I like that. She says what she thinks and doesn't seem to care whether what she thinks will make a person mad.

"I mean, I'm meeting Trout, but he didn't say anything about math homework."

"So Mom's worried about you meeting Trout because he's a troublemaker and you made up a reason, right?"

"Right."

"I see."

"That's what Mom said. 'I see.' What is it with you guys?"

Max was stopped in front of our apartment waiting for Meg, smoking a cigarette as usual.

"Want a ride to school?" Meg asked.

"Nope, I'll walk."

"Suit yourself," she said.

That's another one of Mom's expressions. Meg climbed into Max's red Ford truck.

"Just don't get kicked out of school," she called.

"You can't get kicked out of public school," I said. "It's the law."

"Wrong, Ben. You can get kicked out of any place. Maybe not forever, but for long enough."

"Even though I've got this learning problem?"

"Especially because of that."

The rest of the way to school, I thought about what Meg had said. I'm not a bad kid—not like a juvenile delinquent. I don't break the law, but I am always in some kind of trouble at school, like the invisible cream. Not bad, but just enough to give me butterflies. There's always the thing I didn't do right or say right. I come to school with unfinished homework or I get punished for lost papers or talking out in class or arguing or falling out of my chair or writing notes during homeroom.

The thing is, I *try* to be good. It's as if I can't help

myself, as if there's some other person inside my skin. And he's the guy with learning disabilities who can't sit still.

Trout was standing at the corner waiting for me. He was carrying a large plastic bag from my mother's drugstore and drinking a grape Slurpee.

"So here's the deal," he said, motioning for me to follow him. We stopped just beyond a grove of trees in the park next to school and Trout dropped the plastic bag on the ground and opened it.

"Look," he said.

I looked.

The bag was full of Super Balls. There must have been a hundred of these tiny bouncy rubber balls in reds and yellows and blues and greens. I'd never seen so many in my life.

I like Super Balls. I have a few at home, like three or four, and I like to lie on the couch at the end of the day, bouncing a Super Ball on the hardwood floor to see if I can get it to hit the ceiling.

"So whaddya think?"

"About the balls?"

"Cool, right?" Trout asked.

"Yeah, pretty cool," I said. "They must have been expensive."

"Forty-nine cents each. I put them on my father's credit card," Trout said.

"He lets you have his credit card?" I asked.

"Of course not, banana brain." Trout raised his eyebrows. "I took it out of his wallet this morning while he was taking a shower," he said. "Don't worry. I'll put it back tonight."

"And he won't notice?"

"He's got plenty of credit cards," Trout said, slinging the bag of Super Balls over his shoulder, heading in the direction of school. And I followed him.

Trout didn't tell me his plan for the Super Balls until we were standing in the corridor outside homeroom and he was stuffing the bag from the drugstore into his locker.

"So this is what we're going to do." He shut the door to his locker. "Just before lunch when the bell rings and everyone is rushing down the hall to the lunchroom, we stand on the steps leading to the library and dump the balls in the hallway."

"All of them?"

"All of them."

"So what happens?"

"So there'll be all these balls bouncing down the hall and all these kids running to lunch and it'll be very funny."

"Not if we get caught."

"We won't get caught." Trout leaned on my shoulder. "We'll ask to be excused to go to the bathroom just before the bell, like eleven forty-five, and no one will notice. The hall will be empty and then the bell will ring and we'll dump the balls just as the kids are dismissed for lunch. Get it?"

"I get it."

"And you'll help me out, Ben?"

I didn't answer right away. I didn't know if I really wanted to dump Super Balls in the hallway between homeroom and the lunchroom. It seemed pretty easy to get caught in the first place, and in the second, it didn't sound funny enough to get into trouble.

I couldn't decide until fourth period, when we have advanced reading. Fourth period, the Super Ball deal was sealed.

Everyone, including me, has advanced reading even though I really should be in "behind reading" instead of advanced, but there is no behind. Ms. Ashford teaches advanced and we read long books at home, one chapter a night, and we have a discussion in class. I don't like Ms. Ashford and I don't like reading discussions and I usually don't even read the chapter, unless Meg or my mom has time to help me out, since reading is hard for me. If I do read the chapter, I will have forgotten what I read by the time I've finished because I'm such a slow reader. By the time I'm at the end of the chapter, I can't remember the beginning. And that's just the way it is. Which is why I don't like Ms. Ashford, because she always calls on me first just to be sure to embarrass me, knowing very well the trouble I have reading long books.

So we're supposed to be reading the second chapter of this book called *Holes*. I've already read the first chapter and I liked it a lot, but last night I completely forgot about advanced reading, so today, when Ms. Ashford called on me, I mumbled something about forgetting and she said something like, "How are you ever going to learn to read, Ben, if you don't do your assignment?"

"I forgot," I said.

"That's my point," Ms. Ashford said, and she looked at me with her eyes half closed, as if she couldn't stand to see me with her eyes wide open. "You are always forgetting."

That's when I told Trout I'd do the Super Balls with him.

Lunch for fifth and sixth grade is at twelve and the bell rings at eleven-fifty and it takes a few minutes for everyone to be dismissed and head to the lunchroom. So at eleven forty-five by my watch, after I had finished correcting my vocabulary test and handed the corrections in to Mr. Baker, I asked to be excused to go to the boys' room.

"Trout has already been excused," Mr. Baker said.

I was sitting in my chair and started to wiggle so he'd know how much I had to go to the bathroom. Then he said, "Okay, Ben, hustle up. And since the bell's about to ring, go straight to lunch."

Trout was already standing on about the seventh step to the second floor with his bag of Super Balls. The stairs to the second floor are at the end of the corridor, and all of the fifth- and sixth-grade students have to walk by this staircase in order to get to the lunchroom, which is at the end of the hall.

Trout was completely relaxed, his chin in his hand, watching down the hall where our classroom is, waiting for the bell.

"You stand right next to me, and when the bell rings, we wait two minutes and then, like lightning, we turn the bag upside down so the Super Balls spill out, and you're going to die laughing."

I looked up the stairs to the second floor, where the principal's office is located, and the younger grades and the library, straining to be sure no one was walking around, and to my great relief, no one was. I was actually excited. My heart was beating too fast and my mouth was dry and I was suddenly very glad that Trout wanted to be my friend. That he had chosen me. Someone brave enough to have a tattoo of a question mark on his chin.

When the bell rang, Trout stayed absolutely still.

"How do you know it's two minutes before you should dump the balls?"

"I've done this before," Trout said.

"Super Balls?"

"Yup."

"And what happened?"

"I'll tell you at lunch," Trout said.

And just then, the kids from five and six began pouring out of their classrooms and we dumped the balls, and suddenly the hall was a jumble of moving color and kids were heading through the maze of rubber balls and the building rang with laughter.

"Follow me," Trout said the minute the balls had hit the floor below. "Don't look."

I couldn't help myself. He had left the drugstore bag on the seventh step, and when I looked, it was lying there in a pile of white plastic.

"Shouldn't I get the bag?"

Trout shook his head.

"It'll call attention to us," he said, leaning over the top railing, looking down at the mass of kids running through bouncing Super Balls, and laughed.

"Look, Ben," he called to me.

And I was laughing and laughing.

"Let's go down and check it out," he said.

"Not me," I said.

So we watched from the steps. We weren't alone. A

bunch of other kids from the fifth and sixth grade had run over and were looking down the stairwell at the commotion of kids rushing through the clouds of Super Balls. Mr. O'Dell came flying down the stairs behind us from his office, calling, "Quiet. Quiet everybody. Get yourselves under control."

And then he stood in the hall with his hand on his forehead. There was nothing he could do. The balls were out of control and so were the kids.

"So tell me what happened when you did it before," I asked Trout at lunch.

He shrugged. "Nothing."

"Were you living in Georgia?"

He shook his head. "Mississippi," he said.

"And you did it alone?"

He gave me a fishy look. He had opened his peanut butter and jelly sandwich and was scraping off the jelly. "I lied," he said under his breath.

I wasn't sure what he meant.

"I never did the Super Ball thing before. I read about it in a games book last night and so . . ."

"You don't think we'll get caught, do you?"

"You asked me that already. Who'd catch us?" Trout asked crossly. "No one was in the hall to see anything. I checked."

I walked home alone that day. Trout had tutoring and

Meg had choral practice and I don't really have a pile of friends. That's the trouble with learning disabilities. I'm kind of quiet and a nice guy and I don't push other guys around and don't complain. But most of the time while the other kids in my class are hanging out together, I'm in tutoring. Besides, kids don't like to hang out with a guy like me who's always in what my dad calls "hot water." They think it's funny when I fall over backwards in my chair or spill my milk all over the lunch table or make farting noises in my armpit during library. But they don't exactly want to spend time with me. It's like they think learning disabilities are catching.

That night my parents left straight after dinner for Back-to-School Night. I wasn't worried. I mean, I wasn't any more worried than I usually am when it's Back-to-School Night and I know my parents will come home looking unhappy because of the news they will have heard from my teachers about me.

But it never occurred to me that the story of the Super Balls would be the subject of Back-to-School Night.

I was very glad to see them go because I wanted to call Trout and talk about today. I had the apartment to myself. It was a Thursday night and Meg would meet Max for dinner after choral rehearsal, and then they usually stayed parked in Max's car about four buildings up the hill from our building until eleven o'clock, which is her curfew. So tonight I was alone.

Trout and I talked about everything. About Tim Burger trying to jump over the balls and knocking over Ms. Pratt, the music teacher. About Bucky Freeman sticking a Super Ball down the front of Molly's T-shirt. About Tom Stockdale putting two Super Balls in his mouth like a chipmunk. About Mr. O'Dell trying to get control of the pandemonium and finally calling Ted Stringer, the head athletic director, because he couldn't get the kids to shut up.

"Shut up!" was what he said to us, so you can tell how mad he was.

We talked about everything, from the minute the balls scattered through the hall to the final bell.

"Wait," Mr. Baker had called. "If anyone in this class is responsible for the mess before lunch today, I hope you'll tell me privately." And then he added, "I can promise you that by tomorrow we will know who did this."

"So do you think they know who did it?" I asked Trout for the hundredth time.

"They don't have a clue."

"Maybe someone saw us."

"I've already told you, I'm a professional at this kind of thing," Trout said.

"Maybe Mr. Baker knows."

"No one knows, Ben. Don't worry. Don't even think about it."

I wasn't really thinking about it. I was too excited. Nothing like this had ever happened to me. For a long time, I had been alone at Stockton Elementary and now I had a partner. Trout and I matched. We were like best friends and brothers and twins all at once. That made me feel at home in school, which I hadn't felt since kindergarten.

When my parents came home from Back-to-School Night, I was lying on the couch in the living room watching TV. Actually, as soon as I heard them coming up the stairs, I turned off the TV, which I'm not allowed to watch during the week, and pretended to be studying my vocabulary words at the kitchen table.

"Ben?" my mother called when she opened the front door.

"I'm in the kitchen," I replied. "Studying."

I didn't look up when my father came in the kitchen, opened the fridge, and got himself a beer.

"Want a beer?" he asked my mother.

She didn't. She didn't come in the kitchen either as she usually would, sit down at the table with me, tell me what had happened at Back-to-School Night. My father would talk to me about the meeting too, even though he's less interested in my grades than my mother is and doesn't believe I have as many learning disabilities as my mother does.

"What's up?" I asked.

I knew right away I shouldn't have asked.

"I don't know, buddy," he said. "Nothing good."

I hate it when he calls me buddy and I know he does it because he's angry, sometimes about other things but mostly about me. So right away I figured there was a problem at Back-to-School Night.

I put my vocabulary words in the book bag and took out my math book, opening it as my father left the kitchen.

They were in the living room, but I couldn't hear them talking. One thing about my parents is they talk and talk and talk to each other about everything—dinner and oil in the car and the party they went to and the color makeup my mother likes to wear and my father's relationship with his mother, who is not the grandmother of my dreams, and Meg and me. I can hear them in their bedroom, which is across the hall from mine, talking before they go to sleep. Sometimes when they're having a conversation, it's hard to get a word in "edgewise," as my father would say.

I sat very still at the kitchen table, even holding my breath so I couldn't hear my own breathing, and listened. But I heard nothing. So they were just sitting, probably on the couch or my mother on the couch and my father in the big chair across from the TV. Of course, I couldn't study my vocabulary words, but I did get up and got a carton of French vanilla ice cream out of the freezer and scooped some in a bowl and poured some M&M's over the top. Just as I sat down to continue my make-believe studying, my mother called "Ben?" and she meant it.

"What happened today in school?" she asked when I'd slid into the wicker chair across from the couch where she was sitting.

"Nothing much."

"Does the word 'Super Ball' mean anything to you?" she asked.

My stomach felt as if it had exploded inside my skin and soon I would die.

She didn't wait for me to answer.

"Mr. O'Dell tells me that you and Trout came to school with about a hundred Super Balls today and threw them all over the hall where the lunchroom is and people got hurt—a teacher got hurt, for example." She took off her glasses and wiped her eyes. "And there you have it, Benjamin. Another wonderful Back-to-School Night for your parents."

"That's not the point, Jane. You know that," my father said crossly to my mom. "We have to find out what happened today and help Ben with the mess he seems to get himself into."

"If you insist," my mother said, "but I'm at the end of my rope, Ben. You've got to understand. This has been going on with you since the first grade."

"I have a learning disability," I said quickly, before I even thought what I was going to say. "I can't help it."

"Of course you can help it," Mom said.

"Let's bag the question of a learning disability and figure out what went on today."

So I surprised myself. I told them about Trout and me and the Super Balls. It's not that I lie to my parents when I'm in trouble, but sometimes I stay quiet and let them think whatever they want to think. But suddenly I wanted them to know how funny the Super Balls bouncing through the halls was supposed to be. I told them how funny it was, which it was, and I said I wasn't sorry that I'd done it and that the teacher hadn't been injured at all and that Trout was my best friend. Which is not what my mother wanted to hear.

The truth is strange, especially if telling it is going to cause a problem. At first when I was talking to my parents, I felt wound up tight as a rubber band, as if I were going to propel in the air and fly out the front window. And then, somehow as if confessing the truth is medicine, I began to feel better, even good. Especially glad to tell my mother and father that Trout was becoming my best friend. The first I'd ever had.

My father got up for another beer and gave my mother

a look that said "Be careful," but my mom didn't pay attention. I guess she was too angry.

"The first thing that happened tonight when we walked into the auditorium for Back-to-School Night is Mr. O'Dell met us at the door and told us you couldn't *afford* to be involved in pranks during schooltime."

"What does that mean—afford?" I asked.

I had already decided that I wasn't going to be beaten in this conversation with my mother. That I wanted to fight back. That I didn't really think I'd done anything wrong.

"I think *afford* means if you don't get your act together, you'll be kicked out of school."

"Good news," I said.

"Not exactly, Ben," my mother said. "Then I saw Mr. Baker. After the meeting with all the parents, during which we heard what each class had done this year and how you were all ready to go on to the sixth grade, Mr. Baker asked if your father and I could remain afterwards, he needed to talk to us. In front of everyone, he said that."

"I hate Mr. Baker," I said.

"Mr. Baker wanted to talk to us about Trout and the influence he's afraid Trout will have on your school performance."

My father sat down with his second beer.

"What do you mean, influence?" I asked.

"Trout has had real problems in other schools, Ben. Real problems."

"Like he's a juvenile delinquent."

My father hesitated.

"Exactly," my mom said.

"We don't know that, Jane."

"I know it," Mom said.

"Enough." My dad got up and spilled his beer, which had been sitting on the edge of the couch, kicked the newspaper, which was lying on the floor, and asked my mother to come into the kitchen, he wanted to talk to her.

My parents fight. Not all the time, not even very often, but they do fight. I've never been worried about their fighting because it's over before I have a chance to worry. But they usually don't fight about me.

I decided not to go in the kitchen, where they were talking, and not to call Trout, which is what I wanted to do, of course. So I went into my bedroom, got into my pajamas, turned out the light, and lay on top of the covers, waiting.

Someone must have seen us and told Mr. O'Dell, I thought. Maybe Mr. Baker even guessed that we were "up to no good," as my dad would say. Maybe the librarian or even Mickey Suter, who I had seen go into the boys' room after I had left, and then I forgot to watch the bathroom door to see if he came out while I was standing on the stairs with Trout.

What Trout and I did wasn't terrible. It caused some confusion. Of course, someone had to pick up the balls, but that turned out to be all the fifth graders, so it wasn't a big deal. Ms. Pratt fell down, but she's only about twenty-two and she's soccer coach after school and I'm sure she falls down all the time. Besides, she didn't get hurt.

What I'm trying to say is, we weren't criminals.

I was waiting for one of my parents to come into my bedroom to kiss me good night. I hoped it would be my father. I love my mother, but she gets insane when I have a problem in school. That doesn't happen with my dad. I wanted him to say what he usually says: "Listen, Benjamin, no big deal."

But as it turned out, it was my mom, and worse than that, she had been crying.

"Hi," I said quietly.

"Hi, Benjamin." She sat down beside me on the bed.

"It wasn't a big deal," I said.

She didn't reply. In the light from the streetlights, I could see she was looking away, looking out the window across the street to the market where we get our groceries. It was beginning to seem as if she was going to stare at the market all night when she turned to me and took my hand and said we'd talk about it in the morning.

"What I want you to understand, Ben, and I know it's

hard to understand, but you must make your own decisions about what you'll do. You can't be influenced by other boys, like Trout, who want a partner in crime."

"I did make my own decision, Mom," I said.

"I don't know Trout and he might be wonderful. He might become a very good friend to you. But at the moment, he has come to Stockton with a very bad reputation."

"He told me that."

"Tonight, some of the parents at the meeting said they did not want their children to be around Trout. They said he was too odd. He isn't polite to the teachers and he's got that foolish question mark on his chin just announcing that he wants to cause trouble and he's looking around for pranks like the Super Balls. These parents, and there were several of them, think he's becoming a destructive influence and they want him put in the other section of fifth grade or sent into special education."

"He's not a destructive influence, whatever that is. He's really nice, Mom. Really nice."

"I'm glad he's nice, Ben, but it worries me that the parents of the fifth graders will begin to think of you and Trout as a team."

"We are," I said. "A team is exactly what we are."

She got up from the bed and put her hand on my forehead, but she didn't kiss me, and then she left the room.

"When'll Meg be home?" I asked, but she had gone and I already knew the answer.

77

CHAPTER SEVEN

I don't know how it happened, but by May Day, when we have this big ceremony at Stockton and all the girls dress up and dance around the maypole, I was in tutoring every day. Even during the maypole dance, I was sitting at a desk on the second floor, listening to the music outside and trying to concentrate on what the tutor was saying about fractions. Trout was too, except we had different tutors.

Every day got to be the same. I'd meet Trout at the corner before the first bell. Then we'd go to homeroom and then to classes, where one teacher or another, all except Mr. Worth in science, who seemed to like Trout and me, would have something to say about us that wasn't what we wanted to hear. During recess, we'd have tutoring. The same during lunch. Eat quickly and meet the tutor in the library. No time for recess then either. And after school, we'd have tutoring some more at the place downtown where I've gone since second grade. Since we didn't have the same teachers for tutoring, Trout would be one place bored to death and I'd be another bored to death, and then we'd have a few minutes to talk before the next class. Some days I thought I would go crazy.

Which brings up another problem. I had to see a psychologist. This happened after the Super Balls. The principal and Mr. Baker and my mom and my dad had a meeting and somehow it was decided that once a week, on Friday afternoons after school, I'd talk to Dr. Fern. I didn't have any interest in talking to Dr. Fern. I had nothing to say to him. But apparently that didn't make any difference, since the plans had already been made for me to see him. So on Fridays I'd go to Dr. Fern's office and sit in a chair across from him, and he'd ask me how I was and I'd say fine. And then he'd ask me what I meant by fine. Speaking of dumb questions. Fine means fine, right? And anyway, it was none of Dr. Fern's business how I was.

Trout saw a psychologist too. A woman named Dr. Berriault, who had quite a lot of hair growing out of her chin, according to Trout. When Dr. Berriault asked Trout how he was feeling, he said, "Not so good." In fact, he said, "I'm thinking of setting fire to Stockton Elementary some Saturday when I have nothing better to do." As a result of that conversation, Trout saw Dr. Berriault three times a week after tutoring, which meant that most days he didn't get home until six o'clock and he never even got to play sports or hang out or go to the drugstore for candy.

So it should have been no surprise that we decided to skip school on May 3 and go to New York. This time it was my idea.

We were sitting on the steps behind the school and it was a Tuesday, raining and cold. We weren't even talking. After an hour and a half of tutoring, plus school, plus a meeting with Mr. O'Dell about my behavior and a meeting with Ms. Pratt about my behavior, I didn't want to talk to anyone. Not even Trout.

"My dad's out of town again," Trout said.

"So does that mean you're staying home alone?"

"Yup," he said.

"Creepy," I said. "I mean, I'd be afraid, I think."

"No reason," Trout said. "I live in an apartment, fourth floor, no one's going to try to get in. And my dad has this woman who lives next door that he kind of likes named Ginger, who checks in on me like every hour."

I'd never been to Trout's apartment. We'd been friends for a few weeks and I hadn't been to his place or met his father and I didn't really know anything about him except he was an only child and his mother lived in Hawaii with her boyfriend.

"So maybe we can go to your place," I said.

"To do what?" Trout asked.

"You know. Hang out."

"Not today," he said. "I'm not allowed to have people over when my father's not there. It's the only rule I have except no smoking."

"So if we skipped school tomorrow, we couldn't go to your place, right?"

Trout gave me a thumbs-up.

"Skip school, huh."

"Why not?" I shrugged.

"You're right. It isn't a lot of fun around here."

"And what difference does it make whether we go to school or not? We're still going to be dumb."

"Right. We're the dumbest kids in the fifth grade. Maybe we'll end up being zookeepers. That's what my dad says to me when I get bad grades. 'You'll end up as a zookeeper if you're not careful, Trout,' he says."

"What does a zookeeper do? Take care of animals?"

"Not a chance. A zookeeper shovels manure."

"Sounds fun."

Trout was drawing on the blacktop with a piece of chalk that he'd taken from homeroom. "Stockton sucks" is what he'd written.

"So? Whaddya think?" I asked.

"I think we should skip school and take a train to New York."

New York. I hadn't even thought of New York. I'd been there, of course. Once a year as a treat around Christmas, Meg and I go to New York with my parents, and sometimes we go to the Bronx Zoo, where I want to go, or FAO Schwarz, where I used to want to look at toys when I was little, or ice-skating at Rockefeller Center, where Meg likes to go, or to an art gallery for my mother and a play for my father and then we come home extremely late. I usually fall asleep on the train.

I like New York a lot but I've never thought of going there by myself. I mean, I'm only eleven and not exactly a world traveler.

"Have you ever been to New York?" I asked.

"Nope," Trout said. "I don't even know how far away it is."

"An hour."

"That's not so bad."

"We could leave for school and meet at the corner like we usually do and then walk to the train station, so we'd be in the city by nine-thirty maybe and then hang out till about three and come back."

"Cool," Trout said.

I could tell that he was a little nervous about the idea.

"How long is your dad going to be away?" I asked.

"Till tomorrow night."

"So it'd be easy. My mom and dad go to work when I

leave for school and they work all day till six and then they get groceries and come home and we eat dinner. They'll never know the difference."

"So you wouldn't have to be back till six?"

"Right," I said.

Trout sat on the step with his chin in his hand.

"What would we need to do?"

"Call in sick."

"They'd recognize our voices, don't you think?"

"I can disguise my voice," I said.

"What about tutoring? How many tutors do you have tomorrow?"

"Two," I said. "Ms. Afram for reading and Mr. Bart for math."

"I only have one," Trout said.

"Tutoring will be easy to cancel. We'd call the office and no one will know our voices."

"What about Meg? Do you think she'd call for us?"

"I don't know," I said. "I'd have to think about it."

"Maybe you should ask her first and then call me when you get home," Trout said. "It makes me feel weird to call myself."

On the way home, I thought about skipping school. It made me happy just to think about it, to imagine meeting Trout at the corner and walking to the train and getting on and getting off in New York City like we were regular grown-ups with jobs in the city and no time for school. And then I thought I could actually say I was sick and my mother would call school and notify the tutors. Maybe I could close the bathroom door and pretend to throw up. Who would know the truth? And even my mom understands you can't go to school with the stomach flu. Then I'd have to call her a couple of times during the day so she'd think I was at home. And Meg could call in sick for Trout. I'd tell her Trout's father was away and could she call to say that Trout had the stomach flu too. As long as Meg and Mom didn't talk. It wasn't a foolproof plan, I thought as I walked up the steps to our apartment. But it had possibilities.

No one was at home when I got there so I had time to call the station for schedules on New Jersey Transit into New York City. There was a train at 8:20, which got to New York at 9:20, and one coming home at 4:17, so we wouldn't be cutting it too close in case my mother decided to come home from work early.

I called Trout.

"It'll be easy," I said, and told him the plan.

"That sounds okay," he said. He sounded a little more excited than he had.

As soon as I hung up from Trout, the telephone rang and I thought it was Trout calling me back, but it was my mom at the pharmacy.

"I'm so glad you're there, sweetheart," she said.

As soon as she calls me sweetheart in that maple-sugar voice, I know she's going to say something I won't like.

"What's up?" I asked.

"I've got a doctor's appointment for you this afternoon and I called the school to tell you about it, but you'd left already."

"I'm not sick."

"I know you're not sick. Dr. Fern wants to see you."

"I see Dr. Fern once a week on Friday, Mom. I'm not going to see him any more than that. Already I see him too much."

"I'll pick you up in ten minutes," my mom said, and when I started to protest, I heard the click. She had hung up the phone.

Dr. Fern sat in a chair in one corner of the room and my mother sat on a couch with me and my father sat in a chair next to the couch.

"How come I didn't know about this?" I asked.

"We just found out, Ben," my dad said.

"What did you just find out?"

"Your parents called me after the school called them this morning," Dr. Fern said. He's a small man, not much bigger than me and kind of funny-looking with a gray crew cut and a pointy beard and cowboy boots. I don't like him and I especially don't like the way he tries to be so incredibly pleasant, listening to me carefully as if I'm the most interesting boy he's ever met. Which I know I'm not. He's faking it. He's paid to fake it. Paid a lot, according to Trout.

What Mr. O'Dell had called my parents about was my uncontrollable behavior. I just don't get it. I feel completely in control of my behavior, which I think is excellent. Well, okay. No worse than anyone else's. At least no worse than the boys'. The girls act like girls, so they're always "picture perfect," as my dad would say. But according to Mr. O'Dell, I interrupt classes, call attention to myself, annoy the other students. Mr. O'Dell goes on and on.

"There's a medicine called Ritalin," Dr. Fern was saying.

"I know about Ritalin. I won't take it."

"I think it would be good for you to try it, just for a few weeks, to see if it helps your concentration."

I didn't know why he was worried about my concentration since I wasn't at all worried about it, and already my mother and father had said they were "dead set against Ritalin."

"I won't," I said.

"Just hear me out, Ben," Dr. Fern said.

"Nope," I said. "Either I can concentrate without medicine or I'll end up as a zookeeper."

"Why a zookeeper?" my mother asked as we were leaving Dr. Fern's office.

"Maybe I like to shovel manure," I said.

My dad laughed and ruffled my hair and said this whole nightmare would be over in a heartbeat, and not to worry about the medicine or anything else. Everyone had learning disabilities. Just look at him.

On the way home, my mother got the prescription for Ritalin at her own pharmacy and handed me the pills with the information about them, which pharmacists have to give a person when they order medicine. So I opened the package and read the information about side effects from Ritalin sitting in the back seat of our car.

" 'This medicine is a central nervous system stimulant,' " I read out loud. So you see I'm a perfectly good reader if I'm not nervous in front of a teacher or the kids in my class. "It's going to cause a lot of problems for me. Like, listen to this. They don't *know* if it's excreted in breast milk and I'm going to have to cut out drinking alcohol."

"Going to be pretty tough on you, especially the breast milk," my dad joked.

"And it's going to make me sick. Listen to this— 'check with your doctor if you experience a rash, itching, fever, joint pain.' "

"Benjamin, they have to write everything on the information leaflet. These things almost *never* happen."

" 'Weight loss, irregular heartbeat, blurred vision,' " I went on.

My dad couldn't help himself. He was sitting in the passenger seat looking out the window, trying to hold in his laughter.

" 'Seizures.' Now seizures is something I really need, since I have so much trouble concentrating."

"Oh, Ben. Get a grip," my mom said.

" 'Involuntary muscle movements or changes in mood or personality.' Is that what you want? A brand-new Benjamin Carter, new personality, new mood. *Mom*."

"We're dropping the subject for now," my mom said. "I'm getting a headache."

She always gets a headache when she doesn't like the conversation.

But my parents did decide we wouldn't talk about Ritalin for a couple of days. We'd wait until I calmed down, which wasn't exactly about to happen. Then, as my dad said, we'd discuss the "pros and cons."

"Some guys I know flush their Ritalin down the toilet," I said. "Which is what I'll do, just so you know."

After dinner, I called Trout.

"I'm skipping tomorrow. No question. It's a done deal," I said.

And I told him about the Ritalin.

"I'm not going to a school where they make me take medicine to come there."

88

"Flush it down the toilet like I do," he said.

"I will, but I still hate it that the school treats me like I'm some kind of freak."

"Yeah. Me too. But you'll get over it. They've thought I was a freak since I was six. I don't even think about it anymore."

"So you're up for going to New York tomorrow?"

"I think I am."

"Well, I'm going whether you do or not," I said.

"What about calling in sick?"

"I'm just *not* going to school," I said.

"What are you going to tell your parents?"

"I'll call them from New York so they won't worry."

"Oh, brother," Trout said. "We could be suspended."

"I thought you were the one who didn't worry about that sort of stuff," I said.

"I've just never been to New York before," Trout said, but he agreed he wasn't *so* worried and we decided to meet at eight on the corner of Peartree and Euclid, two blocks from school, and head to the train station from there.

"Bring money," I said.

"Do you have any?"

"I've got about a hundred dollars saved and more in the bank," I said.

"I don't know how much I've got," Trout said.

"I'll lend you some," I said, and hung up the phone quickly when I heard my father coming into the living room.

My dad wanted to talk to me about Trout. He sat down on the couch, put his feet up on the coffee table the way he does, and said he was getting some bad vibes about my new friend Trout.

"Like what?" I asked.

"It seems a group of parents are getting together and trying to get Trout into a special school."

"I know about that. So you're getting to be like Mom and think I shouldn't hang out with him?"

"Just tell me about him, Benjamin. I trust your judgment."

"Mom doesn't."

"That's not true. She's just worried about you. Before spring vacation you were beginning to get on top of things at school, and in the last three weeks, since Trout arrived, we're getting telephone calls from your teachers almost every day."

"It's not Trout's fault," I said, and told him everything I knew about Trout.

"The school worries that his father travels and leaves him at home alone."

"Someone named Ginger in the apartment building

where they live checks in on him. Like every five minutes. That's what Trout told me."

"But he's eleven, Ben."

I shrugged.

"You don't go over there after school, do you?"

"Nope," I said. "But I'm not going to stop being his friend. I like him. I told Mom that Trout is the only friend I've had since first grade who I trust completely. I mean, he never thinks I'm stupid."

"Well, I'm glad about that," my dad said, giving my shoulder a gentle punch. "That says a lot."

"So you don't mind that we're friends?"

"I don't mind at all as long as you just let me know things about him."

"Yeah," I agreed. "I'll keep you up to date."

That night I couldn't sleep a bit. All I could think about was New York and going alone on the train with Trout and walking through the city just the two of us, like we were grown up. And about Ritalin.

CHAPTER EIGHT

It was "a piece of cake," as my dad would say. I met Trout at exactly eight at the corner of Peartree and Euclid. Actually, Max and Meg dropped me off there because I was late. I think Mom had a second sense that something was going on, and after breakfast she kept asking me questions about my math homework and whether I was keeping up in my chapter books and whether I wanted to go to a lake in New Hampshire for summer vacation after I finished tutoring. I was so anxious to get out of the house I didn't even argue about tutoring. But by the time we had finished talking, it was too late to meet Trout, which is why Max drove me.

Trout was waiting, sitting on a brick wall in front of a house on Euclid, but Meg didn't see him and I was glad of that. I didn't want her to tell Mom for any reason, especially since we were just skipping school, not bothering to call in an excuse.

I had about a hundred dollars in my pocket, and we walked to the train station and made the 8:20 New Jersey Transit easily, and the best thing was that I didn't see anyone I knew on the train who might call my parents or the school. Everyone knows my parents, especially my father, since he owns the hardware store. So plenty of people know Meg and me too. But Trout and I were lucky. All strangers on the train, as far as I could tell.

We went into the first car, sat down in one of those double seats so Trout was across from me, and we were feeling pretty great until the conductor stopped to collect our tickets and gave Trout a long once-over look and asked him why he had drawn a red question mark on his chin.

I had pretty much forgotten about Trout's question mark. We were always together, and now when I looked at him, I didn't even see the question mark. Or if I saw it, I wasn't aware. At school, for some reason, the teachers decided to ignore it, even the librarian. Sometimes one of the kids would say something or make a joke but not very often. So I was surprised when the conductor noticed.

"It's a tattoo," Trout said, and he looked startled.

"A tattoo. How old are you?"

"Eleven," Trout said. "Him too." He indicated me.

"And why aren't you in school on a Wednesday?"

"We go to private school and we have a field trip today to the Bronx Zoo and we're meeting our class there."

"Just the two of you eleven-year-olds going to the Bronx Zoo alone?"

"Our school is in a different town and we live in Stockton, which is why we're going by train."

This seemed to satisfy the conductor. He took our tickets and gave us a receipt and moved on to the next passengers, but not without telling Trout he ought to get the tattoo removed, young as he was and with such a nice-looking face.

"Weird," I said.

Trout didn't say anything. He just sat in the train looking out the window as the New Jersey towns whipped by, his arms folded across his chest. I couldn't tell if he was having a good time or not. He was too quiet.

But just after Newark, when we could see the New York skyline with all the skyscrapers like building blocks in the distance, he sat on the edge of his chair and pressed his face against the window.

"So what do you want to do first?" I asked.

"Go to the Bronx Zoo," he said.

Even I was a little scared when we got to Penn Station in New York. It's so big and I had to ask how to get out of the place where the trains stopped and into the station. Then once we came up the stairs into the station, it seemed so much bigger and stranger than it ever had when I came in with my parents. There was a lot of construction and I couldn't tell which way the signs were pointing and I suddenly realized that I didn't know New York at all. I didn't know where I'd be if I followed the signs for Seventh Avenue or Madison Square Garden or the subways. So we went to a desk marked INFORMATION and asked how to get to the Bronx Zoo.

The man told us to take the number 2 express and get off at Pelham Parkway and walk. He pointed us in the direction of the number 2, which meant that we walked underground, which I'd never done before, or if I had, I didn't remember how terrible it was. Homeless people along the walls sleeping, sometimes on green garbage bags with all of their possessions beside them, and musicians playing their guitars or flutes or clarinets, and all the people rushing. There were kids, but none of them seemed to be alone as we were, except one group, and they were traveling with their teacher.

"Are you worried about being murdered?" Trout asked.

"Nope," I replied. I hadn't even thought of being murdered. The only thing on my mind was finding my way to the zoo, but now that Trout had mentioned it, I started to think how easy it would be for someone in the crowd to grab one of us or both of us—no one would notice—and take us someplace and we'd be gone. My parents might never know what happened to us. Just disappeared.

"We're not going to be murdered," I said, but I didn't like the subway, not the smell of it or the crowds of people.

"So you know where we're going?" he asked.

"I do," I said, and I had been following the signs for the number 2, but once we got there I didn't know how to buy a ticket. So I went to the token booth and asked. I got four tokens and went through the turnstile and stood next to a pillar, waiting for the train.

"It'd be easy to push someone onto the tracks," Trout whispered. "I've read about it."

"What did you read?" I asked. I don't read the newspaper and Trout probably doesn't either. It's hard enough to read large print.

"I read that this guy pushed this girl in front of a train. She was just standing there drinking a Coke and he gave her a giant push and she flew right in front of the train and the Coke spilled all over and she was killed and he got away. So."

"Nothing's going to happen, Trout."

I told him to stand by the pillar in case someone did decide to push him; he'd have something to hold on to.

The number 2 express charged into the Thirty-fourth Street stop and we pushed our way into the train with about a hundred other people and had to stand forever until we finally got a seat, and then it was almost Pelham

Parkway. But we made it. We got off the train, asked directions, walked two blocks, and there we were at the entrance.

I looked over at Trout. He had the funniest smile on his face like the "cat who swallowed the canary," as my father would say. It was a great smile and I knew he was having a good time, and to tell you the truth, I was pretty proud of myself. For a kid with learning disabilities, I'd managed to find the Bronx Zoo without getting murdered or pushed onto the subway tracks or getting my money stolen. Not bad for eleven.

By the time we got to the zoo, it was eleven and warm, so we stopped at the lunch place and got hot dogs and two Cokes to cool off and sat down at one of the tables looking at each other. We just couldn't stop laughing.

We were at the zoo until almost three and I've never had such an amazing time in my life, in my *whole* life, and that's been a lot of time.

We kept congratulating each other for being so smart and grown-up.

"It's amazing we're here," Trout said. "I mean, New York City, and we got here by subway, and now we're walking around the zoo like we're famous. My father would die if he knew."

"Yeah," I said. "Mine too."

We got some turquoise cotton candy and wandered around the open bird sanctuary, but I don't love birds—I mean, they're sort of pretty and boring—so we went to see the lions and then to see the monkeys. The monkeys I love, especially the spider monkey with his tiny fingers and toes, eating and spitting, throwing himself at the glass cage, turning upside down. And the baboons with their big pink behinds. From time to time, I'd throw my arm over Trout's shoulder or he'd push into me, like my dog when she was a puppy and tripped me every time I got up from the couch.

We almost forgot what time it was. Trout noticed it first—almost three by the clock over the lion house, so we were late. Not very late, but late enough that we had to hurry to get to the subway in time to be back at Penn Station by four o'clock for the 4:17 to Stockton. We ran to the Pelham Parkway subway stop, bumping up against each other. If we'd been girls, we'd have been holding hands. But since we're boys, we pushed each other instead.

The number 2 was just coming into the station when we arrived and it was practically empty, so we hopped in the third car, plopped down on a seat for two, put our heads against the back of the seat, and nearly fell asleep. Maybe I did fall asleep and maybe Trout did too, because someplace between the time we got on at Pelham Parkway and got off at Penn Station, what was left of my hundred dollars, which happened to be $87.00, was stolen. I reached in my pocket and it was gone.

At first, I didn't tell Trout. I was embarrassed that I'd been so stupid and I was afraid that if he thought a robber was around, he'd be worried.

We walked through the subway tunnel, through the turnstile, and up the steps into the station. We had almost twenty minutes before the train for Stockton left, which meant it was four o'clock, the time I'd planned to call my mom.

"How much money do you have?" I asked Trout, trying to sound casual.

"I've got $4.50," he said. "I don't know what happened because Dad usually leaves me more than that and he gives Ginger a bunch in case I need something, but I didn't want to ask Ginger, so that's all I've got."

I wondered if $4.50 would be enough money to call Stockton.

"So maybe I could borrow some," I said, stopping at the line of public phones.

"Sure," he said, but he gave me a funny look.

I put twenty-five cents in the phone and called the operator and asked her could she help me to get my dad at 609-555-9475, which is the number of the hardware store. At the last minute I decided not to call my mom. She had probably never skipped school in her life, but I bet my father had and would understand.

"Hi, Dad," I said when he answered.

"Just a second," he said. "I have a customer."

I could hear him talking to someone and then he was back on the phone speaking in a quiet voice I'd never heard from him before, even when he was really mad.

"Where are you, Benjamin?" he asked.

I "cut to the chase," as my dad would say.

"I'm in New York and I'll be back at five-twenty on New Jersey Transit and then I'll walk from the station," I said. "I'll be home in time for dinner."

I made it sound as if it was perfectly normal to spend a school day in New York City, as if it wouldn't bother my parents at all. At first, when I got him on the phone, I was very proud of myself. After all, I'd managed a whole day on trains and subways and in New York City and also the Bronx alone with only Trout, and I was the one in charge. But my dad didn't seem to feel that way.

"As you might imagine," he was saying, "the whole school knows that you and Trout cut classes today. Teachers, kids, parents, every bloody person around. This was not a smart move, Ben."

"Okay, Dad," I said, not wanting to let Trout know my dad's mood. "I'll see you at dinner."

"So what'd he say?" Trout asked.

"Nothing much. Just the usual stuff of coming straight home."

"And he didn't mind that you'd gone to New York?"

"He didn't say he minded," I said.

"No kidding." Trout seemed surprised. "So let's get a couple of milkshakes before we go, okay?"

"Sure," I said.

And we headed off to the yogurt and ice cream stand in the station.

The call to Stockton had cost $1.65, which meant that Trout had only $2.85 left. I looked at the price list on the wall behind the ice cream kiosk. A milkshake cost $2.50.

"Let's split one," I said.

"I want a whole one. Chocolate with whipped cream."

"I don't think I want one," I said.

"How come?" he asked.

"I'm full."

"Full? We had almost nothing to eat except a hot dog and Coke and that was a long time ago. I'm starving to death."

I shrugged.

"Is your money all gone?" he asked, suddenly guessing the situation. "Is that why you needed mine to make a telephone call?"

We ordered one chocolate milkshake with whipped cream and shared.

"Yeah," I said quietly. "I think it was stolen."

"Stolen?"

"Maybe on the train. I don't know."

"So there was a robber."

"I guess."

"And he put his hand in your pocket and took your money and you didn't even feel it?"

"I don't know," I said. "When we got to Penn Station, I reached my hand in my pocket and it was gone."

"Jeez," Trout said as we ran down the stairs to the New Jersey train to Stockton. "Do you think that's bad luck?"

"I hope not," I said. "I mean it's bad luck it happened but I hope it doesn't mean bad luck for us."

"Right," Trout said. "That's what I was thinking."

CHAPTER NINE

The day after Trout and I went to the Bronx Zoo, I arrived late to school with my parents because Mr. O'Dell had called the night before to ask us to meet with him at ten o'clock during fifth-grade recess. He said I was not to come to school before ten.

"What does that mean?" I asked my parents at breakfast.

My mother didn't say anything. My father shook his head.

"I don't know, Ben."

No one had said very much to me about skipping school. My parents hadn't even asked about the day in New York and how I'd gotten there and how I'd found my way to the Bronx Zoo. I was disappointed. I expected them to be angry, but I also thought they'd be impressed. I was impressed with myself and so was Meg.

"I can't believe you did what you did, Ben," she said when she came into my bedroom that morning.

"It was easy."

"I mean, New York and all the way to the zoo by subway. Pretty amazing."

"Yeah," I agreed. "I guess I'm not so dumb after all."

She smiled.

"You're actually pretty amazing. Kind of like Dad," she said. "You just don't know it yet."

That's why I like Meg so much. I mean, what older sister in the world says that kind of stuff to her little brother?

"So I hear you've got to go see the principal," she said, brushing her hair in the mirror over my dresser.

"Like, what else is new?" I said. "Mom and Dad didn't say a word about my skipping school yesterday. Dad wanted to know how I got to the zoo, but that was all. And now I'm told not to go to school until ten to see Mr. O'Dell. It doesn't sound good."

"Are you worried?"

"I don't know. What can Mr. O'Dell do? I'm already in tutoring all the time and I'm sent to his office about every other day and I spend at least one day a week after school in detention. I guess I could go to jail."

"That'll be next week," Meg said, and she tossed me a bag of peanut M&M's and left for school.

It was almost eight when Meg went downstairs to meet

Max and I called Trout. I expected him to answer the phone as he always did, but his father answered.

"Trout isn't here," he said. "He's gone to school. Is this Ben?"

I wasn't expecting that and my heart flip-flopped when he mentioned my name.

"Yes," I said.

"Trout's in a lot of trouble and I imagine you are too," he said.

"I guess," I said. I could hardly breathe. It's not that Trout's father sounded mad. Worse than mad. He sounded huge, as if in person he was a man twice the size of my father or Mr. O'Dell or any other man I knew. His voice was big, and mainly it was the sound of his voice that scared me.

"I'll tell Trout you called," he said, and hung up.

Mr. O'Dell called attention deficit disorder a disease. "The symptom of the illness is that a child can't pay attention or sit still."

We were sitting in his office. I was on the couch with my mom, and my dad was in a chair across from Mr. O'Dell's desk and he looked furious every time Mr. O'Dell opened his mouth. I've never seen my father lose his temper, but I was thinking maybe he'd lose it at Mr. O'Dell. That would be nice.

"I don't believe it's fair to call it a disease, Mr. O'Dell," my father said. "That'll make Ben think he's ill, and he's not."

That's the trouble with Mr. O'Dell. He thinks he knows everything. He probably thinks he could be President of the United States if he had some free time. And what does he know about diseases? He's a principal and not a doctor. Not even a very good principal. So he doesn't know anything about diseases. He doesn't even know that he's mentally ill. At least that's what Trout and me think.

I happen to know a lot about attention deficit disorder, since I was told I had it when I was seven. Even though my father says I'm a perfectly normal boy, I know my mom is right when she says I have more trouble sitting still than other kids, especially girls. So maybe I do have ADD and maybe I don't.

But I don't plan to take any medicine. Every morning, unless I have a cold or the stomach flu, I get up and feel great. If you feel great without medicine, why take it? Right? That's what I told my mom and dad and Dr. Fern and Mr. O'Dell, when Mr. O'Dell said to my parents that I had to go to a special school.

"Does that mean you're kicking me out of Stockton?" I asked.

"It means I want you to try Ritalin as Dr. Fern recommended, at least for the remainder of the school year, which is less than six weeks," Mr. O'Dell was saying.

He went on to say how half the boys in the world take Ritalin, even his own son, like that will change my decision. I know his own son. He's a grade ahead of me and he's a weasel.

"Otherwise I'm kicked out of public school?"

"If you can't get control of your behavior, you need to be in a place where you'll get some help."

"Like where?"

"Brazillier Learning Center is where some of the children from Stockton go to school until they can catch up with their peers."

Brazillier Learning Center is a place for dummies worse than me and Trout. Three boys in my class have gone there in the last two years and one girl. It's on the other side of town and I couldn't walk there and I wouldn't have any friends unless Trout got sent too and so I made a quick decision about Ritalin.

"I'll try Ritalin," I said. "I mean, I won't die from it," I told Mr. O'Dell straight off, as if I'd really changed my mind, that sure I'd try Ritalin.

This made Mr. O'Dell very happy and he thanked my parents for coming in and said that in no time he expected to notice a *great* improvement in my behavior. That almost all of the children on medication showed improvement, and some turned into excellent students, like his very own stupid son.

I smiled, or at least I think I smiled, and said I was

sorry about skipping school and I certainly wouldn't do it again. Which wasn't true. I'd do it in a heartbeat.

As for the Ritalin, my parents promised I'd never have to take a single pill.

I met Trout at my locker. He was waiting for me.

"I guess you know what happened," he said.

"To you or me?" I asked.

"To me."

"I don't know anything except Mr. O'Dell says I'll have to go to a special school unless I take Ritalin," I said.

"I'm being switched to the other fifth grade," Trout said. "Mr. O'Dell told my father that I was becoming a bad influence on other boys in the class, especially you."

"Yeah. Right."

"So you and I need to be separated, is what Mr. O'Dell said. And also that some of the parents won't let their kids play with me."

I shrugged. "Stupid parents."

"It doesn't make any difference," Trout said. It wasn't as though he was about to cry. He was quiet but not upset. Maybe mad. Maybe he was mad at me.

And I don't blame him since my stomach sort of fell when he told me he was moving to the other fifth grade.

"I'm really sorry about changing classes," I said. I told him that he was my best friend. I've never had someone I thought of as my best friend unless it's Meg. So maybe Trout was the second.

"I'm not coming back here tomorrow. I probably won't ever come back," Trout said, and he lifted his book bag on his shoulder and left.

I called after him, but he didn't turn around, just kept on walking down the corridor and out the front door of the school.

I hurried, hoping to follow him, but by the time I got outside, he was gone.

I walked to tutoring alone. Usually Trout and I walked together, talking about how we hated school and how we wished we were grown up and then we'd talk about what we'd do if we *were* grown up. Trout wanted to buy a Toyota truck and drive to California. I wanted to be smart.

"How do you think you'll suddenly turn smart?" Trout asked.

"It could happen."

Most of the time, I believed that I was smarter than people thought. My parents told me that, my dad especially. He said that people, especially teachers, didn't know me very well. If they did know me, they'd know that I'm just not regularly smart like A students. One day, my dad said, I'd wake up in the morning and my brain would be on a fast track and I'd be able to do all of my school-work without thinking about it.

I crossed Main and headed downtown past the pharmacy to the tutoring building. I was hoping to see Trout. Usually on Thursday, we'd go together and then go to my mom's drugstore and buy some candy. But I didn't see him ahead of me, so I guessed that he'd probably gone home. That he'd decided not to have tutoring any longer and maybe his father had decided they should move again. It made me sad to think about.

And then just as I was walking up the steps to the tutoring building, I saw him. He was across the street, sitting on the ground at the edge of Stockton Park, leaning against a tree. I waved, but he may not have been looking.

So I crossed the street and walked along the sidewalk until I came to the place where he was, and sat down on the ground beside him without saying a word since he didn't seem to want to talk.

It was three-forty-five exactly. I had forty-five minutes of reading with Ms. Sutton. So now I was skipping tutoring. I didn't even feel guilty.

We sat for a long time without talking. I saw Ms. Sutton come to the front door of the building and stand on the top step looking around for me.

"There's Sutton," Trout said finally.

"Yeah."

"So you're not going to reading?"

"Are you?"

"Nope," he said. "It doesn't make any difference anyway."

We stayed like that for a while. His tutor, Mr. Grady, came out of the building, got into his car, and drove away.

"Did you cancel?" I asked.

"Nope," he said.

The sun began to dip behind the tree and, without it, the air was cooler and the ground under us felt damp. From time to time, I glanced over at Trout and he hadn't moved. He sat with his knees up to his chest, his chin resting on his knees, staring across the street.

"So what're you going to do?" I asked.

It was almost time for tutoring to be over for me, and my mom would be expecting me at the drugstore just to check in. Meg was taking me out to dinner, since it was my parents' anniversary and they were having dinner alone.

"Nothing," Trout said.

"I mean, are you going home soon?"

"Nope." He reached in his pocket and took out a pack of Parliament cigarettes. "Want one?" he asked.

"Sure," I said.

He opened the package and took out one cigarette for me and one for him.

I don't know whether I had ever held a cigarette before. My parents don't smoke. My grandparents don't smoke. Meg doesn't. Max does, but he's never offered me a cigarette.

I took it. Trout had put his in his mouth between his lips right in the middle. I did the same.

"I don't smoke, so I don't have a match," he said.

"S'okay," I said.

So for a long time we just sat there smoking unlit cigarettes.

"Do you know how to inhale?" Trout asked.

"Nope."

He breathed in very deep through his lips.

"Like that," he said. "I'm not supposed to smoke because cigarettes kill you."

"I know," I said.

"But they have to be lit to kill you, right?"

"I think," I said.

I wasn't sure. I actually have never been interested in smoking cigarettes, but I liked sitting on the ground with Trout and pretending to smoke. It felt friendly, as if it was us against the world.

"So what do you think's going to happen to us?" he asked.

"Nothing. I mean, you'll change to the other fifth grade and I'll say I'm taking Ritalin and throw it in the toilet, and then school will be over and we'll have a great time this summer."

Trout said nothing.

"Isn't that what you think?" I asked.

"I don't know," he said.

I was looking at him sideways. Close up in daylight I could see the cracks in his tattoo, little bits of skin showing through the red. I don't know what I was thinking, maybe nothing at all, maybe about the tattoo.

"I'm going to wash it off," Trout said.

"I thought it was permanent. A tattoo. That's what I thought it was."

"I lied," he said. He licked his finger and rubbed the red question mark just at the bottom so the red came off on his finger. "See?"

I didn't say anything. I didn't know what to say. There was suddenly something different about Trout, something old. As if he'd grown up while he was sleeping last night. He seemed quiet and silent, not unfriendly but not particularly friendly either. Not stuck to me like Velcro as he had been.

"Do you want to come over to my house?" I asked.

"Your parents hate me."

"My parents don't hate you."

"They will. Pretty soon they'll hate me like the other parents do because I'm disturbing your work like Mr. O'Dell says and getting you in trouble. I know all about that because Mr. O'Dell had a meeting with me and my father this morning."

"My parents have no reason to hate you. They love me and I'm in as much trouble as you are."

Trout shrugged. "That's the way it is," he said.

We stayed there until I could feel that it was starting to get dark, and it wasn't until I checked my watch and saw it was five o'clock and knew I'd better get home that Trout began to talk.

He told me about his mother first. How his mother had gotten a boyfriend and moved to Hawaii and left Trout with his father when he was seven years old.

"Do you visit Hawaii?" I asked.

"Once when I was eight," he said. "It wasn't fun."

"Hawaii wasn't fun?"

"My mom really didn't want me there. She wanted to hang out with her boyfriend, so she kept saying didn't I want to go home early and I said no and so I stayed. But she didn't ask me the next year. She comes to visit on Christmas, but that's all. And now she has a new baby."

He told me about his father and how his father is a salesman and travels a lot and changes jobs and moves to different towns. Every time Trout moves to a new school, it's okay for exactly a week and then he's in trouble again.

"So I don't have friends because kids are afraid they'll be in trouble if they hang out with me," he said. "Or," he went on, "maybe they don't even like me."

"And since you move all the time, you don't have time to make friends."

"Right." But he was thinking of something else. "It's not just that we move all the time because my father gets a new job. We move because I get in some kind of trouble at school and my father gets embarrassed because I'm not perfect or the school says I have to go to a special school and then my father looks for another job in another place. So it's my fault, sort of," he said. "At least, that's what my dad says."

The end of my cigarette was getting too wet, so I turned it around and pretended to smoke the other end. I didn't know what to say to Trout. His story was the saddest story I'd ever heard. I began to think that here he was, my best friend, and I hadn't known anything at all about him, not about his mother or his father, and worst of all, not about the terrible life he'd had.

"I think you should come with Meg and me to dinner tonight," I said. "It's my parents' anniversary, so they're going out together."

Trout didn't answer right away. He thought about it and then he decided that it'd be okay since Meg wasn't my parents and so we walked to the corner of Euclid and Main and he used the pay phone to call his father. His father must have said no because Trout said it didn't make any sense for him to go home unless his father was going to be there for dinner, too, and why should he stay home alone. And that he'd be home by eight or his father could pick him up at our apartment.

Meg took us to a Japanese restaurant called Mikado, where you sit on the floor and eat with chopsticks, and we sat in the back of the restaurant at a small table on the floor, just the three of us, and we talked. I was surprised. Trout told Meg all the same stories he had told me and told her that his tattoo was a fake. He drew it on with Magic Marker every morning and washed it off at night. He told her about his learning disabilities and flushing Ritalin down the toilet at night. And then he said he was never going back to Stockton Elementary again. All he did was skip school one day and now they were changing him to the other fifth grade and next year he was being sent to a school for dummies.

Meg listened quietly. Every once in a while, she got a sad look on her face and she'd touch Trout's arm or shake her head or say how awful his life sounded. Then she had a plan.

The plan was simple. Every morning we'd meet at the corner like we already did and walk into school together, promising each other to be quiet and well behaved all day long. For every hour of the school day we were not in trouble, Meg would give us a surprise. And so, if there were eight hours of no trouble, that meant eight surprises.

"What if one of us is bad and not the other?" I asked.

"No surprise. That's the deal," Meg said. "It's up to both of you."

"It's a deal," Trout said.

And "that was that for this," as my father would say.

CHAPTER TEN

Meg's plan worked. At least we thought it was working. We didn't miss tutoring. We didn't interrupt classes or get sent to Mr. O'Dell or have to sit outside the classroom for rudeness or talking out of turn. We even did all our homework.

Every afternoon at around five o'clock, we'd meet Meg, sometimes at The Grub and sometimes at home, to tell her about our successful day. And she'd get us our prizes. One day it was eight M&M's each. Another day, it was eight stickers each. Another, it was eight pencils. And once it was eight cents each. So we thought we were doing really well.

But as it turned out, we were wrong. I don't understand how things happened the way they did. But they did.

We should have caught on. That's what I said to Trout later.

I mean, the first week of Meg's plan, Billy Blister had a birthday party and invited all the boys in the class, at least all the ones I know except for Timbo Wirth, who's a juvenile delinquent, and Trout and me.

"So did you get invited?" I asked Trout at recess, when all the boys were talking about Billy's birthday party.

"Nope," he said. "Billy doesn't like me."

"Well, he likes me and I didn't get invited."

Trout shrugged.

"Maybe he forgot."

"Maybe," I said.

I didn't ask Billy how come he didn't ask us, although I wanted to. But Mary Sue told me on the way home from school one day that she heard Billy was having an all-boys birthday party and I wasn't invited and neither was Trout because of the parents.

I shouldn't have asked Mary Sue anything since she has such a bad character, but I couldn't help myself. I wanted to know.

"What about the parents?"

"Billy's parents," Mary Sue said. "They said you couldn't come because Trout is such a bad influence on you. A lot of parents feel that way."

"Wrong," I said. "Trout isn't a bad influence on anyone."

But later that night, after Meg had given us our prizes for good behavior, I did ask my mom what she thought I

118

should do. And she asked my dad and he said he couldn't stand the way people are like sheep and move around stupidly in herds and never think for themselves.

"What does that have to do with Billy's birthday party?" I asked my mom when she came in to kiss me good night.

"Just that some of the parents of the kids in your class don't understand Trout, so they don't want their children to play with him."

"Idiots," I said.

"I think so too. But what happens is one set of parents tells another set of parents about Trout and on it goes, and pretty soon everyone is telling his son not to play with Trout. It's very sad and wrong."

I decided not to tell Trout what my mom or Mary Sue said. Already he had enough unhappiness with his mother in Hawaii.

During the second week of Meg's plan, Mr. Baker called my parents to say how well I was doing now that I was taking Ritalin. Which I wasn't, but my parents didn't give Mr. Baker that information.

"Just like I used to say to you, Ben," my mom said. "It's *your* behavior. You ought to be able to change it without taking medicine. Or at least it's worth a try. And you have."

The next day Mr. O'Dell called me in to the office to tell me how well he thought the Ritalin was working.

I would have liked to tell Mr. O'Dell that it was all me

by myself making the difference in the way I behaved. But I didn't.

"So I wanted to see you today about Trout. Not you. How's that for a change?"

"Good." I didn't trust Mr. O'Dell for a millisecond. He always had something up his sleeve.

"Trout may be leaving Stockton Elementary at the end of this year."

"He didn't tell me," I said.

"He didn't?" Mr. O'Dell asked.

"Nope. We already planned some stuff we're going to do next year in sixth grade like try out for the traveling soccer team. I mean, he didn't tell me anything about leaving."

"Well, he will."

"How come he's leaving?" I asked.

"To go to another school. At least that's what I've heard from his father."

"Nobody told him," I said.

"What I wanted you to know is that I think sometimes you are left out of things like birthday parties because some of the parents are concerned with the lack of supervision at Trout's house."

"I don't understand," I said. "That doesn't have to do with Trout. That's his father's fault."

"I just thought you should know."

And then we talked about other stuff at school and what it would be like to be a sixth grader, but I forget what we said since all I was thinking about was telling my dad what Mr. O'Dell had told me.

That night my dad said Mr. O'Dell shouldn't have said anything about Trout to me. It was unprofessional. "Bad character" is what my dad probably thought, but he didn't say that.

"So what're you going to do?" I asked.

"Call him," my dad said. "He should be fired."

"Roger," my mom said.

"I mean it, Jane."

"Are you going to tell him that?" I asked.

"Probably not. But I am going to tell him he shouldn't be speaking to my son about another student. Those matters are private."

"Are you going to tell him I'm not taking Ritalin?" I asked.

"Of course not. It's not his business."

Later that night Trout called me and said he might have to change schools.

"How come?"

"My dad says that Mr. O'Dell wants me to go to another school."

He sounded as if he might be crying and Trout doesn't cry about stuff.

"What school?"

"He didn't say anything to me. Maybe he told my dad.

But something weird's going on at school, like the more I try to do well, the worse things are."

"I thought things were great," I said. "I mean, we're hardly ever in trouble."

"I know," Trout said. "But my dad says things aren't going very well. That a lot of the parents of fifth graders think I'm a criminal."

"A criminal?"

"You know, like a criminal. Not a guy they want their kids to know."

And then last Saturday, there was an end-of-the-year picnic at the Baileys' farm and Jonno Bailey said to me I could come but his dad didn't want the responsibility for Trout, because the Baileys had a lot of animals and farm equipment and just about anything could happen with Trout around.

"What do you mean by that?"

"You know, accidents," Jonno said. "Stuff like that."

"No problem," I said. "I can't come to the picnic anyway." But I thought about Trout and what was happening to him for no reason, how he was getting blamed for being a boy he wasn't. It was kind of scary, especially now that he was trying so hard. Like me. As if Trout and me had been chosen to take the blame for all the bad things that happened.

* * *

And then on Monday night, the last week of May, two weeks before the end of school, some of the parents in the fifth grade called a meeting with Mr. O'Dell at Mary Sue Briggs's house and invited all of the other parents, including mine and Trout's father.

The meeting was about Trout.

"What do you think has happened?" I asked my dad.

"I'm not sure," he said. "Remember I told you about this group of parents trying to get Trout moved to a special school?"

"I remember."

"They have a 'bee in their bonnet' about Trout for some reason."

"What'll happen?" I asked my mom.

"You guys have cleaned up your act," she told me. "I don't think anything will happen. What can the parents do if nothing is wrong? Answer me that."

But I was still worried.

Monday night, Trout came for dinner.

"We can't just let him sit home by himself while this meeting is going on, since he knows he's the subject of it."

"How did he find out?" I asked. "I didn't tell him."

"Mr. O'Dell called his father and his father told him."

My parents went to the meeting early, but they got

123

take-out for us and we sat in front of the TV eating lasagna and waiting for Mom and Dad to come back. I don't even know what was on TV, we were so upset. Especially Trout.

So we just sat there side by side picking at our lasagna, which was kind of glumpy and cold, waiting for the bad news. I don't remember if we talked much. Probably not.

But at nine o'clock, just about the time we were expecting my parents to come home, my dad called.

"I've got a proposal for you, Ben," he said. "And you've got about two minutes to think about it."

The meeting was not going well, he told me. The things the parents had to say about Trout weren't true and weren't fair, but it made no difference. They were a large group and they could very well force Mr. O'Dell to send Trout to a special school for children with emotional difficulties.

"Do you know what I mean by emotional difficulties?" he asked me.

"I think I do," I said. "I think it means to be upset and a little crazy."

"That's right," he said. "Do you think Trout is upset and a little crazy?"

"He's upset because people are mean to him. But I think he's normal, I mean as normal as me. Just a kid with learning disabilities."

"That's what I think," my dad said.

"He hasn't really done anything terrible, Dad. Just pranks."

"And he's different. Sometimes people take off against a kid who's different. They're looking for kids all made from the same jelly mold. You're not like that and neither is Trout."

"You mean, it's not that he's done bad things, but they're afraid he could *do* bad things."

"That's right, because he's not just like their child, so they don't understand him. And someone needs to tell the fifth-grade parents that he's a great kid, just a little different than some of the other fifth graders."

Which is when he gave me his proposal.

"A person who knows Trout very well needs to speak to the parents. Someone who might help change their minds about him."

"And that would be me?"

"That's what I'm hoping, Ben."

"You mean, come right now and talk to a bunch of parents without even having a speech written to read."

"That's what I mean," he said.

"What should I say?" I asked, my blood turning to thin water.

"Say what you believe, Benjamin. That's all you can do."

CHAPTER ELEVEN

I'd never been to Mary Sue Briggs's house and I've never even wanted to walk down Magnolia Street, where she lives, which has the largest, richest houses in Stockton, New Jersey. Her father is a lawyer and works in New York City and her mother spends the day at the country club. That's what I've heard. But it was kind of exciting to drive past these mansions, *huge* mansions, with wide green lawns and tons of flowers, and to walk up the flagstone sidewalk of the house where my worst enemy lives with her parents and her fluffy dog.

On the drive over, my dad and I didn't talk, although his hand was on my knee the whole time until he parked the car.

"Will everyone be there?" I asked.

He nodded as I followed him up the front steps and

into the marble hallway of the Briggses' house, where a long table of tea and coffee and cookies was littered with old cups and crumbs. The meeting had started at seven-thirty and it was almost nine-forty-five.

There was a wide stairway with steps going up either side as if a person needs two sets of stairs to go to the second floor. At the landing, the fluffy white dog sat looking down at us. I imagined that Mary Sue was lying on her stomach on the top step straining to hear the conversation at the meeting, but I couldn't see her.

"We'll go in," my dad was saying to me, "and I'm going to sit down at the back where Mom is and you'll just walk down the middle of the living room, which is long, to the fireplace, and stand there to speak. People have been waiting to hear you and I'm sure Mr. O'Dell is still there and he'll probably say something like, 'Here's Ben Carter.' Okay?"

"Sure," I said. I didn't want to sound afraid. And I wasn't nearly as nervous as I would have been if I had had time to think about talking to a bunch of fifth-grade parents in front of Mr. Baker and Mr. O'Dell and worst of all my own parents.

"Trout's father is here. You know that."

"Yeah, I know that."

"Have you met him?"

I shook my head. It was strange. I'd never met his

father and I'd never been in his apartment, and here we were, best friends.

"There." Dad pointed as he slipped into the back row next to my mom.

I only saw the back of Trout's father, but I could tell he was tall like Trout with that silky flying hair, only gray. I looked at him when I walked through the rows of parents, some sitting on the floor, some in folding chairs, but he didn't turn his head to look at me, just sat facing forward, his arms across his chest.

Mr. O'Dell was sitting beside the fireplace talking to Ms. Briggs, who has yellow hair that she wears in a pony-tail as if she's fourteen years old. I think Mary Sue will be just like her when she gets to be forty or sixty or however old Ms. Briggs is.

"Here comes Ben Carter," Mr. O'Dell said, standing up beside the fireplace. "Hi, Ben."

I didn't respond with "Hi, Mr. O'Dell." This wasn't exactly daytime TV.

"Ben and Trout have been great friends ever since Trout came to Stockton. The best of friends. And I'm glad he's here to tell us about the Trout he knows."

Mr. O'Dell has a way of talking that makes me want to throw up, so I kept my eyes straight ahead and didn't look up. All I could see were his feet.

The parents were restless, moving around in their chairs,

talking back and forth, so I wasn't walking into silence, which would have made me very nervous. In fact, no one seemed very interested in me until I stepped in front of the fireplace.

"Do you need a microphone, Ben?" Mr. O'Dell asked.

"No thank you," I said, and at that moment, it was as if I'd had a huge glass of super-vitamins and there was a whoosh of power like the ocean in my blood.

I told the whole story of Trout and me, but I started with Mary Sue Briggs and the drowned teddy bear. I told the truth and I didn't leave anything out, but I didn't look at Ms. Briggs, although I had a sense of her sitting just beyond where I was standing. I talked about the question mark and how it wasn't a tattoo but Trout *needed* it because he felt invisible without it.

"Trout and I have learning disabilities. It means we spend recess and half of lunch and a free period every morning and after school working with tutors. We are not exactly like the rest of the kids in the fifth grade because we learn differently and sometimes it feels terrible." I could hear my own voice like an echo in a hollow room, and it sounded good and strong and certain. "You feel stupid and uncomfortable. Teachers think you cause trouble on purpose, that you fail at school because you don't try. But that's not true for Trout or for me."

I told them about the Super Balls and skipping school.

About Ritalin and how I wasn't taking it even though everyone thought I was. And I told them about Meg's plan. I couldn't believe my own ears listening to the story I was telling. It was as if the words came from the air.

"Trout Sanger is the best friend I've ever had," I said at the end. "He understands what it is to be in trouble in school when it's not your fault and what it is to be different from the other kids who know how to read and what it is to feel lonely because you're outside the group. He has taught me that I'm a good kid whether I'm smart or stupid."

Everybody clapped. Some people stood and clapped. As I walked through the room towards my parents, people slapped me on the back and said "Good job" and gave high fives.

I didn't hang around. I walked past my parents and straight out the Briggses' living room into the large marble hall and to the front door without looking up the steps to see if Mary Sue Briggs was hanging halfway down the steps trying to listen. I opened the door and walked towards the car.

"I want to go home," I said to my dad, who had followed me out. I certainly didn't want to talk to any of the parents or hear their congratulations or answer their questions. I was proud of myself, maybe not right away, but the next day, when I thought back to what I'd said. But I was also feeling suddenly quiet because I'd told a lot of strangers the truth about me, things I'd always wanted to keep secret because I was embarrassed.

Trout's dad caught up with us as I was getting in the car.

"Ben," he called in a huge, deep voice. He grabbed my hand and then he lifted me up off the ground because he's so tall and hugged me. "Thank you. That was very brave and very kind."

My dad took me home. Mom and Trout's father stayed to finish the conversation about Trout's future.

"So what do you think?" I asked my dad.

"I think you were amazing."

"Do you think they'll change their minds?" I asked.

He was silent, considering.

"I think they will," he said finally.

Trout was asleep when we got home. The television was off and Meg was in her room listening to music, talking on the phone to Max.

I woke him up.

"Want me to tell you what happened?" I asked, already beginning to be full of myself.

He shook his head.

"In the morning," he said.

"He's afraid," my dad told me in the kitchen, where he was making himself a sandwich.

"Of what?"

"Put yourself in his shoes," he said. "He's in trouble,

131

the parents don't like him for no good reason. And there you are, his best friend, talking about him to a bunch of people who don't like him. Not a great way to feel, right?"

"I guess," I said.

"Just go sit down beside him. Maybe he'll ask and maybe he won't."

So I did that and we sat there on the couch, quiet a lot of the time or talking about nothing, kids at school, the soccer team next year, mean teachers. His father brought my mom home from the meeting, but he didn't come up-stairs, so I didn't have a chance to see him again.

"What happened?" I asked my mom.

"All good," she said, kissing me on the top of my head. "Trout will be back next year in the fifth grade and I guess you two guys will be practicing for the soccer team all summer."

Trout said goodbye and went downstairs to meet his father, but he didn't thank me.

"See you," he said, and walked out the front door.

"Don't worry," my dad said when he came in to kiss me good night. "It's hard to know what to say when someone's done you a big favor. 'Thank you' doesn't seem enough. And sometimes you're embarrassed or feel you owe them something back. This was a big deal. Trout's got to have time to think about this."

Still, I couldn't get to sleep for a very long time.

* * *

Trout called just before seven.

"Meet me at the corner," he said.

We always met at the corner of Euclid, every day for weeks, so I didn't know why he needed to call this morning, but I headed out early and was waiting for him when he came up the street.

At first when I watched him coming up Euclid, I knew there was something different. I just didn't know what it was—a different look to his face. And then, of course, I realized the red question mark was gone.

"Is it off for good?" I asked.

He shrugged.

"I don't know. I'm going to a new school next year, so maybe I'll put it back on then."

My stomach fell.

"I thought you were going to be at Stockton. I thought we were doing soccer and stuff together."

"We're moving to New Hampshire," he said. "My dad's got a new job."

I was quiet all the rest of the way to school. I was actually afraid that if I spoke, I'd cry, so I didn't speak and didn't dare look at Trout.

"Did you know you were moving last night when you were over at my house?" I asked finally.

"Nope. He told me this morning."

"So after the meeting."

133

He nodded.

I put my stuff in my locker, got out my language arts book, shut the locker door, and waited for Trout to finish getting organized. The halls were crowded and a few kids from the fifth grade gave me a swinging pat on the shoulder or knocked up against me in a friendly way, so I guessed their parents had told them that Trout and me are okay guys. A couple of kids stopped and talked to Trout too.

"So are we still doing Meg's plan?" Trout asked.

"Sure," I said. There were only two more weeks to summer vacation.

"Maybe today she'll give us eight cigarettes," he said.

"Right. Steal them from Max."

All morning I had trouble concentrating, more even than usual. I couldn't stop thinking about Trout moving away and it made me a little sick, as if I were coming down with the flu.

It wasn't until we were on the blacktop at gym, standing on the edge of the basketball court without any particular plan for something to do, that Trout talked about the meeting with the parents. I could tell that he had something to say, but he didn't say anything until the bell rang and kids started running past us on their way up the steps and into the building.

"So what's up?" I asked.

"My dad told me this morning that I'm your best friend."

"You knew that," I said.

"He says you told everyone in the whole auditorium, all the parents and stuff."

"I did."

"That's what he said."

I gave him a funny look.

"You're weird," I said.

He shrugged.

"I guess you know you're my best friend too," he said. "Even when I move to New Hampshire. I won't get another like you."

It was a hot day and we were standing on the blacktop with sun beating down on us, blinding our view, the last kids on the playground, the final bell ringing.

"We could bolt," I said. "Go someplace like Montana."

"For the day? I've got a dentist's appointment tomorrow morning."

"Yeah, just for the day. We'll be back by dinner."

"Then let's get our stuff and head to Montana," Trout said.

And we raced up the back steps of Stockton Elementary, running into the building just as the last bell stopped ringing.

We went to Montana, just the two of us, a couple thousand miles from New Jersey, rode horses up in the mountains, and then got home in time for dinner. I mean, we were a little late, of course.

"Montana?" my father asked us when we walked in the front door. "That's a long way away. Did you have a good time?"

"We had a great time," I said. "We can go anyplace together, even when Trout moves to New Hampshire."

So I'm not surprised I thought it was Trout on the front steps of Stockton Elementary this morning. We have big imaginations, especially Trout.